Donita Miller

LEI OF LOVE

LEI OF LOVE

•

ANNETTE MAHON

AVALON BOOKS
THOMAS BOUREGY AND COMPANY, INC.
401 LAFAYETTE STREET
NEW YORK, NEW YORK 10003

PRINTED IN THE UNITED STATES OF AMERICA
ON ACID-FREE PAPER
BY HADDON CRAFTSMEN, SCRANTON, PENNSYLVANIA

For Sharon Wagner . . .
    for the honest critiques,
    for the constant support,
    for your unwavering faith in my ability;
    and most of all, for being a friend . . .
    Thank you, thank you!

Chapter One

"B rian?"

Police detective Brian Vieira maintained his appearance of casual comfort as he sat back in his office chair, but his grip on the phone turned his knuckles white and his heartbeat increased by half. Was his mind playing tricks on him? That voice—that wonderful liquid feminine voice that still held the power to make his heart race. He'd never forgotten the sweet molten sound of it, but it had been two long lonely years. . . .

"Brian it's Dana. Dana Long. I . . ." There was a pause as though the speaker found the words difficult to say. "I need your help."

Brian listened for the subtle nuances of her voice, still so familiar even after their time apart, and caught the edge of desperation there. So he replied in what he hoped was his most professional voice.

"Certainly, Dana. Is this about a police matter?"

"I don't know. I hope not."

Brian considered that, considered the worried tone of her voice and the fact that she was calling him at all, and decided it was indeed a police matter.

"Shall I meet you . . . ?" He let his voice trail off, not certain what she expected of him.

"Could you come to my father's house?" There was another slight pause. When she spoke again her voice was quiet, relieved. "Thank you, Brian."

Brian ran her few simple phrases over and over in his mind as he drove the short distance to Isaac Long's home. It had been two years since he'd talked, really talked, to Dana. Two years of bitterness, loneliness, polite nods, and irrelevant small talk when they couldn't avoid meeting. And yet she'd called him now when she needed help.

Brian braced himself as he pulled into the familiar driveway. His restless fingers combed through his thick hair, rearranging the dark waves that insisted on falling across his forehead. Somewhere deep inside a little voice reminded him that he wasn't the only cop she knew. Did she just like to mess up his life? Or didn't their past relationship affect her anymore?

With a burst of frustration at the idea that women could be so incomprehensible to men, Brian slammed the car door.

Waves of memories assaulted him as he mounted the steps to the small porch at the front door. The large hibiscus still grew beside it, its double orange blooms nodding heavily in the light afternoon breeze. Unbidden, a mental picture of himself posing on those steps with Dana appeared.

It had been their college graduation dance, their last real date. He'd felt silly in his rented tuxedo, a grown man of twenty-seven decked out like a kid going to a prom. She'd been so beautiful in a gown of deep pink satin she'd designed and sewn herself. He could almost smell the white carnations in the lei he'd given her, the spicy scent of the maile she'd given him. And he easily remembered the pride in her father's eyes as he stood at the bottom of the stairs and took their picture. He even recalled how she'd laughed, claiming that her bright pink dress clashed with the orange blossoms beside them, insisting that he change places with her. Yet less than a week later—

The sound of the door opening drew him from the past. Warmth flooded through him, a warmth that had nothing to do with the balmy eighty-degree temperature and everything to do with the diminutive woman standing on the porch above him. It was a warmth that threatened to soothe the pain he was clinging to for his self-preservation.

She was more beautiful than ever. Two years ago she'd worn her dark hair long, like dozens of other Hawaiian girls who danced in hula shows. But it was shorter now and the style was definitely flattering. Short curls feathered across her brow and hugged her neck, spiraling into the collar of the soft white cotton shirt she'd carelessly tied at the waist. Her tanned legs were shown to perfection beneath lemon yellow shorts and the toes of her bare feet curled over the edge of the threshold.

Although her dark eyes were clouded with worry, her mouth formed a tentative smile of greeting. Wide and satiny smooth, her lips were an irresistible pull to Brian's eyes. He could almost feel them beneath his own, meeting him kiss for kiss.

Drawing a raspy breath, Brian reminded himself that this was business. He nodded toward her as he entered the house. "Nice to see you again, Dana."

Brian stopped abruptly just inside the room. Surprise and disgust at his opening comment and the sincerity of his voice consumed him. Why on earth had he admitted how glad he was to see her? For two years he'd fought to contain his anger and frustration and hurt. And now the first time they were alone together, the first thing he did was blurt out how nice it was to see her. Perhaps what made it even worse was that it *was* nice to see her again. Brian frowned at his private admission as he stepped into the center of the room.

Dana smiled absently as she gestured toward the sofa, closing the door automatically behind her. Of course she'd seen Brian a few times over the past two years but usually at crowded parties or luaus. She was perfectly aware of how handsome he was. But until now, seeing him up close this way, she hadn't noticed the new gray hairs sprinkled through the brown over his ears. The variation in hair color made him even better looking. More interesting, perhaps—piquing the viewer's curiosity into wondering what had caused them.

Seating herself at the opposite end of the sofa, Dana looked into Brian's familiar eyes. No one had eyes like Brian's, a light clear brown, almost hazel, but with a darker ring around the iris. As she met his gaze, reluctant though it was, the worry that had absorbed her for the past eighteen hours diminished, replaced by a certain faith in Brian's ability to make things right. It was always what he did best.

Realizing that she was quickly falling back into the old pattern and angry at herself for a weakness believed conquered, Dana plunged quickly into her tale, first taking a moment to express her appreciation.

"It was nice of you to come. I didn't know who else to call." Her eyes dropped down to her hands, clasped tightly in her lap. "I knew you'd listen and not laugh or call me silly." Her eyes moved back up to meet his and her lips parted in a grin. "Even if you wanted to."

Brian didn't smile though Dana thought she noted a softening of his expression. Wanting to bypass the awkward moment, she hastened into her story.

"I came over here late yesterday because I hadn't heard from Dad for a couple of days. I thought it would relieve my mind if I stopped over and saw that everything was all right."

Brian raised an eyebrow but didn't interrupt.

"Since I moved out, we've made it a point to talk on the phone every day or every other day—just to chat a moment, and so I can make sure he's okay."

Dana glanced at Brian, but his expression remained the same. She knew he would under-stand, being close to his mother and grandmother. Then a guilty look entered her eyes, and her lips turned down in self-disgust.

"I've been awfully busy lately trying to get the shop ready for its opening, so I haven't been perfect about calling. Sometimes I don't get home until really late. Then yesterday I real-ized he hadn't called me since Tuesday. So I decided to stop by on my way home—surprise him, you know." One slender hand gestured ex-pressively before dropping back into her lap. "Anyway, when I got here yesterday, Dad wasn't here. That in itself is unusual because he's always here at four getting ready for din-ner, which he always eats at five."

Dana clasped her fidgety hands, glad that it was Brian she was telling all this to. He'd seen her at her best—but also at her worst. Unable to keep her hands still, she tugged nervously at the tails of her cotton shirt as she continued her story.

"When there was no answer, I let myself in. And not only was no one here, but the place is a mess. You know my dad, Brian. This house is always neat, with everything in its place. It's not like him to go off somewhere with the kitchen full of dirty dishes and wet towels on the bathroom floor. He didn't even make the bed!"

Aware that she was beginning to lose control, her voice gaining a near-hysterical edge, Dana took a few deep breaths and willed herself to a calmness she didn't feel.

As she talked, Brian's eyes were drawn to her lap, where nerves were causing her fingers to fidget. Brian had always liked her hands. They were narrow with long tapering fingers and perfect oval nails. When she danced they were unbelievably expressive, telling beautiful stories effortlessly.

Even though she was visibly upset, Dana looked great, Brian thought. If anything; she looked better than ever. Two years' time had ripened her beauty, giving her a little more sophistication. He couldn't help but notice as she tugged at her shirttails that her petite figure was still stunning.

He tried to keep his eyes focused on her face and concentrate on what she was saying. The effort caused a thin line of perspiration to gather beneath his hairline, and his hand closed tightly over the arm of the sofa.

Dana didn't notice Brian's discomfort. She was peering into his unusual eyes, willing him to understand why she felt so concerned.

"The thing is, Brian, his stamp collection is gone."

Brian released his breath with a long, low whistle. So she did have a real basis for her concern—something more substantial than the natural concern of a daughter for her father. Everyone who knew Isaac Long—and that amounted to half of Hilo—knew about the gregarious old man's treasured collection of rare Hawaiian stamps. He wondered how many of them also knew that Ike disdained safe deposit boxes and kept the stamps hidden in his home.

"Are you sure?"

"Of course I'm sure." Dana's lips thinned, pulling down at one corner. It was the kind of comment she would have expected of Brian two years ago, but she'd hoped for better now. "I know where he keeps it and I even tried a few places where he *used* to keep it. It's gone, Brian."

Her hands flew out, expressing her frustration and perhaps indicating the direction of her search.

"So this morning, when I found he hadn't returned, I called all our relatives and all his friends I could think of. No one's seen him since day before yesterday."

Brian felt a crazy urge to take her into his arms and reassure her, but that would never do. There was a new maturity present in the actions she'd described. Two years ago she would have called him immediately. Apparently she'd acquired a new sense of independence since their breakup.

Dana returned Brian's regard with more assurance than she felt. His thoroughly masculine presence still had the power to raise her temperature and make her stomach flutter. The faint scent of his after-shave drifted over to her, filling her nostrils with its spicy fragrance and her mind with warm memories. Even her body responded to the familiar balm with a small shiver of longing. Dana realized that more than anything, she wanted Brian to take her into his arms and comfort her. He was so good at that.

Dana gave herself a mental shake. Yes, he had been very good at comforting her. And at directing her life. But she was perfectly capable of running her own life.

Brian ran his fingers through his hair, pushing the unruly waves away from his forehead. Without realizing he did it, he straightened his shoulders and shifted to the left, moving himself slightly away from Dana. He was feeling uncomfortable sitting there so close, yet unable to touch her. She was distracting him so much he was having trouble keeping his mind on their conversation.

Dana watched his shoulders move beneath the loose-fitting aloha shirt and wondered if they'd gotten wider or if it just seemed that way. With great reluctance she pulled her eyes back to his face.

Brian cleared his throat. When he spoke it was in what Dana recognized as his "professional" police detective voice—polite, calm, soothing.

"Well, Dana, I'm not sure what to tell you. As I think you realize, there isn't any real evidence of foul play. With Ike gone we can't be sure the stamps were stolen. You've done about all that can be done at this point, checking with all his relatives and friends. I couldn't have done any more myself."

Dana felt a warm glow at the implied praise and at the admiration she could see in his eyes. It was nice of him to come after what she'd done two years ago, but then Brian had always been a nice guy.

Dana suddenly realized that the silence had stretched into minutes while they stared at each other. Was Brian reminiscing too? Dana clasped her hands in her lap and tried to smile at him. "What do you suggest I do now?"

Brian cleared his throat, took a small notebook and a ballpoint pen from his pocket, and prepared to take a few notes. "Let me have Ike's vital statistics. You know, height, weight, birthdate . . ."

Dana supplied all the information he requested and he made what she felt sure were neat little notes in his notebook.

When he finished writing he flipped the notebook closed. "We'll have to wait until twenty-four hours have passed to start official procedures."

Dana bristled at the official tone his voice had taken. "But Brian . . . No one I talked to has seen him since Wednesday morning. That's over forty-eight hours."

"But you only know for sure that he's been gone since yesterday evening." His voice was calm, perfectly reasonable.

Dana looked at Brian through narrowed eyes. She hoped he wasn't being condescending. With a small frown she realized that she wasn't being quite fair. After all, he didn't have all the facts yet.

"Naomi says the garage has been empty since Wednesday."

She watched Brian digest this fact. He knew as well as she did that Naomi Tanaka, the elderly widow who lived across the street, was a notorious busybody. She spent her days, and possibly her nights as well, sitting at her front window stitching her Hawaiian quilts and keeping track of all her neighbors' comings and goings. And she was unusually reliable in her gossiping.

It was Brian's turn to frown. "Okay, Dana. I'll report Ike missing. Maybe you should stay here tonight, just in case he comes back."

Dana nodded, glad to have an official assignment. "Fine. What else can I do?"

Brian frowned. He thought staying at the house was a full-time job. If this was a robbery and kidnapping, he wanted Dana as far away as possible from the actual investigation. With an amateur robbery gone wrong, there was no telling what could happen. And no professional burglar would have taken an old man with him.

"Draw up a list of all his friends, relatives, neighbors—anyone who might have seen him in the last two days. Include addresses and phone numbers if you can. We may have to check with them again."

Brian rose to leave. That little assignment should keep her quietly busy for the rest of the day at least. He walked to the door, tucking his notebook into his pocket as he went.

"Meanwhile, I'll start things from my direction." His expression softened as he noted once again the fear and anxiety clouding Dana's face. He reached over, running his fingers lightly along her cheek to her chin. "It'll be all right, Dana. He's probably just visiting one of his friends in the country."

Dana felt his light touch all the way to her toes. If it was meant to be soothing, it failed miserably. She felt more agitated than ever. She had to step away from his touch before she could manage a weak smile. Given the circumstances, they both knew it was rather unlikely that Ike was just visiting friends, but it was nice of Brian to try to comfort her.

As Brian stepped through the screen door, Dana called after him. He stopped on the porch and turned to face her, his hand still holding the door open. Dana followed him out and stood on the small porch beside him.

"There's something I have to tell you." Her gesturing hand encountered one of the hibiscus blossoms and she snapped the stem and began to toy with it.

Brian, trying to put some distance between them on the tiny porch, leaned his hip against the low railing and waited for her to speak. Obviously what she had to say was going to be difficult. He hoped she wasn't going to bring up their past.

"It's about Dad," Dana finally managed to blurt out.

Brian found himself oddly disappointed. Not that he wanted to discuss their past relationship. Especially out here on the open porch. Naomi was undoubtedly watching from her front window.

"What about him?" he asked cautiously. Something about her attitude and tone of voice alerted him that Dana was worried about something more than her absent father and the missing stamps.

The fragile hibiscus petals were beginning to shred between her agitated fingers and she tossed the blossom over the porch railing with a sigh. She pushed her hands into the pockets of her shorts and stared at the floor. Her bare toes almost touched the polished tips of Brian's loafers.

"I've been worried about him for a while now." She brought her eyes back up, a beseeching look in their depths as she faced Brian. "It's hard to explain. There isn't any one thing I can put my finger on as an example. It's just that he hasn't been himself, and I'm worried. He forgets things, things you'd never expect him to forget." Her voice was indicative of her frustration at her inability to verbalize the problem.

Dana took a deep breath. The one episode that worried her the most was the one she was most reluctant to share. Even with Brian.

A neighbor had called her, just last week. He'd found Ike wandering through his property, looking confused and asking if he'd seen Rose. Since Rose Long had died some eight years before, the neighbor had been concerned enough to call Dana.

Yet when she arrived at her father's that evening, he was his usual self, finishing his dinner right on schedule and with no recollection of his earlier venture.

Dana stared into Brian's eyes for a moment and then shrugged. She didn't want him to publicize the search as one for a confused old man. "It's kind of hard to explain," she finally repeated.

"Sort of woman's intuition, in other words."

"Well, a little more than that. After all, I lived here with him for twenty-two years."

"I always wondered why you moved out."

It wasn't a question. The words were spoken in a quiet voice, almost as if he were just thinking out loud. But the statement irritated Dana. It was proof that he'd never understood her at all. Her lips tightened as she reined in an irritable reply that she knew she would later regret. She drew herself up to her full height and straightened her shoulders. It made her feel better even though it only brought the top of her head up about even with the tip of his nose.

"Thank you for coming out, Brian. I can't tell you how much I appreciate it."

Brian moved away from his position against the railing and looked into her eyes. He was so near she could feel the heat of his body. His voice was low and sincere.

"You know I'll always help you, any way I can." Surprised at the promise in his own voice, he moved swiftly down the steps. At the bottom he turned. "Ike's a great guy and I wouldn't want anything to happen to him."

Without another word he entered his car, started the engine, and backed out of the driveway.

Dana blinked in surprise at the swift turnabout. He'd sounded so—

Oh, who was she trying to kid. She still cared about Brian—always had, always would. It was the main reason she tried so hard to avoid him. But trying to instill romantic meanings into his statements now that they would be working together would only cause more future heartache. He was helping her because they had been friends at one time and because he liked and respected Ike Long. Period.

Chapter Two

"Dana! That you? You okay?"

"Yes, Aunty, I'm fine. Are you calling about Dad?" Dana sighed quietly, trying hard to be patient at what must have been her two-dozenth phone call since the evening paper reported Ike missing. Friends, relatives, neighbors—everyone wanted to know what had happened and to recount the last time he or she had seen Ike. Dana had spoken to each person, hoping that someone would provide the scrap of information that would tell her where Ike had gone. So far, nothing new had surfaced.

"Wassa matta that brudda mine?"

The familiar lament brought a tired smile to her lips. "Have you seen him, Aunty Ruth?" Although this had happened time and again,

Dana couldn't help the shiver of hope that raced through her at the thought that Ike might have gone to see his gruff but loving older sister.

"No."

Dana's brief moment of hope disintegrated, only to be resurrected at her aunt's next words.

"I saw him Wednesday. Drove right by the house and never even wave. You hear from him yet?"

"No, no I haven't. I've been on the phone the whole time. Ever since the evening paper was delivered. Everyone we know has called, but no one's seen him." Dana readjusted the position of the receiver. "Which way was he going when you saw him?"

Ruth lived just outside Hilo in Wainaku. It might not help at all, but it was the most Dana had so far.

"Away from Hilo. Could have been going any-place."

Dana sighed, audibly this time. He had numerous friends out along the Hamakua coast. He could indeed have been going anywhere.

"Was he alone in the car, Aunty Ruth?"

Ruth replied that he was, and with a further bit of tongue-clicking at her errant younger brother, she said good-bye and hung up.

While the constantly ringing phone did provide a welcome distraction, the frustration at everyone's lack of information was wearing. By the time Dana finally finished up the lists Brian had requested and fell into bed, it was early Saturday morning. She spent a restless night, the jangling phone waking her long before she was ready to get up.

One of the earliest callers was Brian. She was so relieved to hear his voice she felt her eyes grow damp with tears. *It's because I didn't get enough sleep*, she told herself. *I'm too tired.*

His voice carried across the miles, a balm to her sagging spirits. "How are you, Dana? Are you managing all right?"

The warm sympathy in his voice gave her new energy.

"I'm okay. I must have gotten at least a million phone calls, but none of them were any real help. Dad drove by Aunty Ruth's on Wednesday afternoon—didn't even wave, she said."

Brian knew Aunty Ruth. " 'Wassa matta that brudda mine?' " he mimicked. He also knew that the gruff exterior hid a heart as large and soft as a down pillow.

Dana laughed. It felt good to relax and laugh after the tension of the last day. But the problem of her missing parent couldn't be ignored for long.

"She couldn't help as far as where he was going, though, just that he was heading away from Hilo. And, Brian," she added, "he was alone in the car."

Dana could hear the smile in his voice. "That's great, Dana. It means he left on his own, so we can rule out a kidnapping. We won't know about the stamps until we catch up with him, though. Stay there and keep taking those phone calls. One of them will eventually turn up something important. One of them might even be Ike."

"I sure hope so."

"I have a few ideas I'll be following up on this morning, then I'll stop by. If you need me, leave a message at the station."

As she replaced the receiver, a rush of warmth spread through her as the sound of his voice, so warm, so concerned, echoed through her senses. Even over the phone, his power over her was still potent. Determined to overcome such weakness, Dana pulled her mind away from Brian and on to other things. She was in the kitchen forcing down a piece of toast and some orange juice, resolutely checking her initial inventory list for the shop, when the phone rang.

"Dana? Martin Chung here."

Dana smiled at the sound of the familiar voice. Martin Chung was an old friend of her father's who lived out near Honomu. He and Ike had worked together in the state tax department, and had retired at the same time. Together they had decided to take up orchid raising as a hobby. Chung had gone into it in a bigger way than Ike, keeping more varieties and often adding new plants. The two men spent a lot of time visiting back and forth, admiring each other's efforts. Dana had called him several times, but had been unable to reach him. Now she could almost feel the other man's discomfort coming across the phone line as he spoke.

"I'm real sorry, Dana. I just heard on the 'Mynah Bird' show that Ike is missing," he said, mentioning the popular early-morning deejay who'd given the missing person's report on his program. "I'm real sorry I didn't call yesterday, Dana. I had no idea."

Dana's heart jumped at what, in its disjointed way, seemed to be the first real important news she'd had.

"Is he there now?"

"No, no, he was here Wednesday. He came right after lunch. We looked at my new plants. Talked story. He stayed for dinner. Didn't eat much, and it was Patty's chicken long rice." It was obvious from his tone of voice that he thought there was something very strange about Ike passing up this particular dish of Patty's.

"How did he look? Did he say where he was going?"

"He looked okay, but his clothes were kind of rumpled. Not his style, you know. He seemed tired. It was getting dark already, so I told him to stay the night. Didn't want him driving back to Hilo in the dark. He got up real early the next day and left without having breakfast. I'm sorry I didn't call, Dana. I should have realized something was wrong."

"It's all right, Mr. Chung." Dana wanted to be reassuring. There was no reason for Ike's old friend to feel guilty about something like this. "Did he say where he was going?" she asked again.

"No, didn't say where he was going. But he did mention an old army buddy who's supposed to be on the island for a convention. Talked about him and how nice it would be to see him again. You think he went to his hotel?"

Dana's heart leaped with joy. Her first real lead! "Maybe he did. Did he say what hotel?"

"No. Didn't even mention his name actually. Just called him Crazy Cal. I remember him talking about him before but I don't remember his real name."

Dana couldn't keep the excitement from her

voice. "Oh, Mr. Chung, you've been a big help. Thank you so much."

Dana rushed through her good-byes. Calvin Coolidge O'Reilly, aka Crazy Cal, here on the island! She'd heard wonderful stories about his army-day antics ever since she was a girl. She was so excited by this unexpected lead that she had to get out of her chair and pace to calm herself down.

Finally she stopped before the window and stared out at Ike's vegetable garden. Why hadn't she noticed earlier that it wasn't in its usual neat and tidy state? There were weeds between the beds and the birds were eating some overripe tomatoes that hadn't been picked. Two papayas lay rotting on the ground beneath the tree; two others were ready to be picked. The more she looked around the guiltier she felt. She should have seen these things earlier—should have understood they were a sign of something bigger.

Dana chewed her lip while she considered the alternatives. She should call Brian. No. He'd said he would be out all morning. Anyway, she was perfectly capable of deciding what to do without him. She would call the hotels and see if a Calvin O'Reilly was registered.

Over an hour later, when Brian appeared at

her door, Dana was tired but flushed with her recent success.

"Do you have any idea how many hotels there are on this island?"

She saw Brian start to smile before he changed it to a frown. "Hotels? Dana Long, have you found out something you haven't told me?"

His authoritative tone put Dana on the defensive and she frowned back at him. "He's my father, Brian, and I'm worried sick about him." She straightened her shoulders and led the way into the kitchen. "Besides, you were out all morning—you told me that yourself."

Brian gave Dana a look of frustration. It was true he'd been running around all morning, but he'd told her the station would be able to track him down. Perhaps that new maturity he'd sensed the day before was going to be more problem than help.

He accepted a soft drink from Dana with a curt nod of thanks and met her eyes across the table when she sat down opposite him.

"Okay. Tell me what you discovered that had you calling hotels."

Dana looked more animated than she had since this began as she relayed the story from Martin Chung, told Brian something about Cal

O'Reilly, then explained how she thought she'd help out by calling the hotels.

"Only I didn't stop to think about how many there are! My fingers are sore from dialing. But Brian . . ." She looked at him and a wide smile brightened her face, relieving some of the tension that had been present the day before. "I've found him. I've found Calvin Coolidge O'Reilly."

Brian wanted to stay angry at her for taking things into her own hands. He'd specifically told her to report anything important to him, and she'd realized how important this was. But they *had* pretty much discounted a kidnapping. And the way she looked when she smiled . . . She was so lovely and the joy of solving this little puzzle took that unbearable tension from her eyes. Whenever he saw those fine lines gather in the center of her forehead, he wanted to smooth them away with soft caresses and gentle kisses. Just the thought was enough to make his fingers ache to touch her satiny skin, to glide along her cheekbone and down those newly relaxed cords in her neck.

But he couldn't let her know how close she still was to owning his heart. She might discard it just as carelessly as she had once before. So instead of smiling tenderly at her the way he longed to do, he frowned again.

"So where is he?"

Dana saw the frown on his lips and couldn't reconcile it with the tenderness she'd just seen in his eyes. She frowned back at him for a moment before regaining her good humor. "The Mauna Kea Beach Hotel." She rose from the table and took Brian's empty glass. Moving quickly, she put it into the sink and stared back at him impatiently. "Well, come on. Let's go."

Brian's frown deepened. The tenderness left his eyes and he remained steadfastly seated. "Where are *we* going?"

Dana released a sigh of frustration. "Why, to the hotel of course. Mr. O'Reilly is currently out on the golf course with a guest—a guest of his own, not another hotel guest." She paused to be sure Brian caught the significance of this fact. Then she glanced at the clock and moved toward the door. "It's not even eleven-thirty. We can be there by one if we leave right away. The person in the pro shop thought they might finish up anytime after one-thirty."

Brian continued to pierce Dana with his best professional look. "Dana." His voice was patient. "You are not going to the hotel. I told you last night, you can help a great deal by staying right here and answering the phone. You can see how important that is."

Dana tried to control her impatience and her voice was remarkably calm when she spoke.

"That was when robbery and kidnapping were a possibility. But yes, I can see that it's important to monitor the phone. So I had my assistant Malia bring the answering machine I got for the shop, and I've set it up. Anyone who calls can leave a message."

She noticed a spark of surprise pass through Brian's eyes at her initiative. He was going to be more than surprised when he discovered that instead of meekly saying "yes, Brian," and doing as he suggested, she was going to hold her ground.

"Besides, I'm going stir-crazy just sitting here, thinking of what I could have done to prevent it . . ."

"Now, Dana—"

"I know, I know. You're going to tell me it wasn't my fault. But I still feel guilty, Brian. I feel like there were signs here that I missed, that somehow I should have been aware that there was a problem." Her eyes drifted out the window to the neglected garden and darkened with resolve. Her voice was firm when she continued and turned to face Brian head-on. "I *have* to help, Brian, and I'm going to the hotel this afternoon. With you or alone, but I *will* go."

Brian stared at the dark-haired beauty before him. She was dressed casually in shorts with a matching top made from a bright pink tropical print. She'd probably made it herself. It looked like Dana. The voice was hers, soft and melodious. But the words . . . Could this assertive woman really be the shy, agreeable Dana he remembered?

He looked at the determination in her eyes, the resolute set of her shoulders, and decided to admit defeat. Otherwise they might be here for another hour.

He rose from the table. "All right. Let's go. But, Dana." There was a slight warning note in his voice she didn't dare ignore. "You are to do as I say while you're with me."

"Yes, Brian." Dana smiled happily at her success and decided to address any other problems as they arose.

Dana opened the car window all the way, reveling in the cool salt breeze that caressed her face and blew through the thick strands of her hair, lifting the damp curls from her neck. How she'd needed this! To get out, to breath the fresh sea air.

Being in her old home brought too many memories. The possible causes of Ike's disappearance seemed imponderable. The long drive on the beautiful coastal highway was just the prescription to buoy her sagging spirits.

She turned slightly so that she could look at

Brian. He had a strong profile, his chiseled nose just short of being prominent. His marvelous light-brown eyes were often unreadable, which made them mysterious. And his skin was a warm golden brown, the result of both genes and the ever-warm Hawaiian sun. Dana noted a few fine lines showing near his eyes. They went nicely with his graying hair, giving him a very distinguished look, but she hoped they were signs of laughter and not stress. And then there was his mouth. It was a generous mouth, made for laughter and kisses . . .

From the corner of his eye, Brian could see that Dana was staring at him. It made him uncomfortable, yet he was glad that being away from the house was enabling her to relax. She seemed younger and more at ease, as a woman of twenty-four ought to be.

Being alone with Dana in the close confines of his car for an hour and a half was going to be awkward. Awkward, heck—it was going to be downright uncomfortable. He wanted to reach over and pull her against his side, then rest his hand on her leg. It lay there so near, long and slender and barely covered by the brief pink shorts. He could almost feel her cool skin, smooth beneath his fingertips . . .

His wandering thoughts were beginning to bother him. Trying to distract himself, Brian reached over to turn on the radio. Mellow Hawaiian music flowed over them along with the salty sea air.

"What station would you like, Dana?"

"That's nice." Pulled from her own daydreaming by the music of ukuleles and steel guitar, Dana listened for a moment. Almost automatically, her graceful fingers began to move to the rhythm. But as she realized what number was playing, she caught her hands together in her lap and held them tightly clenched. Would Brian recognize it? A quick peek told her nothing. He was looking straight ahead, watching the traffic on the busy highway.

Brian was having a hard time keeping his mind on his driving. His peripheral vision enabled him to see Dana enough to know she'd frozen up at the sound of this particular song. Interesting. Maybe she wasn't as untouched by him as he'd originally thought.

Unable to listen to any more, Dana reached out to turn off the radio, but Brian's hand shot out to stop her.

Pulling her hand back into her lap, Dana realized she no longer felt cool and lighthearted. Painful memories dragged her back too far. Trying to keep her voice even, Dana moistened her dry lips and turned toward Brian.

"I decided I'm not in the mood for music after all."

"I am."

Dana debated reaching for the dial again, decided against it as being hopeless, and concluded that she would have to bear through the number. She remembered all too well the last time they'd heard this together. Brian's cousin's luau for his son's first birthday. It had been a beautiful day, a wonderful party. As everyone filled up on the delicious food, the impromptu musical performances had begun. Eventually Brian had pushed Dana forward and someone had played this number on the guitar. Its beautiful strains had haunted her ever since. For on that day, deeply in love, she'd danced the romantic number for Brian alone. And everyone present had been aware of the message passing between them, so much so that at the dance's end there was a breathless moment of silence before the applause began.

The number on the radio ended and another began. Rhythmic drums led into an ancient chant. Dana knew the chant, had even danced to it. But thank goodness, it had no painful memories connected with it.

Brian's quiet voice broke in on her thoughts. "Why did you give up dancing, Dana?"

Dana looked over at Brian's profile, a

thoughtful expression on her face. "How did you know I'd given it up?"

A long, low chuckle filled the car and flooded Dana with feelings she thought it best not to explore. "You cut your hair."

It was Dana's turn to laugh. Her laughter was softer, more fluid and feminine, and to Brian's mind it created a special music. It made his skin tingle just to hear it.

"Well, Detective Vieira, you're right. I retired two years ago and last summer gave in to a sudden impulse to cut my hair. But I still dance occasionally for a special luau or family party." Her eyes were drawn outside the car to the beauty of the steep green cliffs they were passing as they rounded the second of the great curves near Lapahoehoe. She didn't want to remember special family parties. Her voice was dry as she added, "It was time for me to move on to other things."

Brian waited a moment but she didn't elaborate. He concentrated on the road until they were out of the long curve. "Well?" he finally said. "Are you going to tell me about the other things? I assume you're referring to opening up that shop you've always dreamed of."

From the time he'd first met her as a junior in college, Dana's dream was to have her own small shop. She wanted to design and sew specialty clothing—bridal gowns, prom dresses, hula costumes. He'd always felt the idea highly impractical, especially since she could do the same work from her home. It would take a great deal of capital to start operation and it might be a long time before she acquired enough clients to stay out of the red. His opinion on the subject had been one of the things he felt sure had led to their eventual breakup. But they were no longer together. It really wasn't any of his business if she pushed herself into bankruptcy. He just hoped she wouldn't take Ike along with her.

Dana's initial look of surprise quickly fled. Of course—she'd mentioned the shop casually yesterday and again this morning. She'd hardly realized she'd done it, but a detective like Brian would have noticed and remembered. Dana smiled sadly. She wanted nothing more than to share her dreams with Brian. But these were the same dreams she'd shared two years ago, a major source of contention between them then.

However, they still had a long ride ahead of them and they had to discuss something.

"I know you thought I was foolish two years ago to take that job sewing for Hawaiian Holiday Wear. But I only did it to get some experience in the fashion industry and to save some money. I learned a lot there, especially after I moved into management. And I've been sewing at home too. If I do say so myself, I've been doing pretty well, all by word of mouth. So when Kepola Kelekolio asked me to do the costumes for her *halau* for the Merrie Monarch Festival competition, I decided it was time to go out on my own."

Brian let out a low whistle. The Merrie Monarch Festival was known for its outstanding hula competition, and doing the costumes for the whole *halau*, or company, would probably mean a very nice contract. It was certainly a great honor. And everyone in the hula world would get to see her work.

"I'm very happy for you, Dana."

Dana smiled, pleased that she'd managed to impress the practical Brian. She'd half expected a lecture on the impracticality of her ideas. She knew him well enough to tell he wasn't excited for her, but he was willing to listen and wish her well. It gave her a warm feeling inside to see this compromising side of him.

"It worked out perfectly. Dad has a friend who's giving me a break on a small store downtown. It isn't the best location, with the downtown area dying out, but there are several other nice shops there and a great little restaurant, so I think it will work out well." She went on to tell him of some of the things she'd been doing the past few weeks to get the little store ready to open.

By the time she finished, Dana felt like she'd been talking for hours. But she sensed a new basis of mutual respect that boded well for the reestablishing of their friendship. Feeling better than she had in days, she stared out the window at the cattle grazing lazily in their pastures. Goodness, had they come this far already? When had the fields of sugar cane changed to ranches and pastureland? She'd been so engrossed in their conversation that she'd failed even to notice the miles they'd covered. With a start she realized Brian was addressing her.

"I'm sorry, Brian. What did you say?"

Brian frowned. "Have you eaten at all today?"

"Yes, of course."

Brian raised an eyebrow, a skeptical look on his face. "What?"

Dana resisted her first impulse, which was to tell him it was none of his business. Of course it *was* none of his business, but he still seemed to feel some obligation to look out for her. And because some small part of her still welcomed that protected feeling he could give her, she answered. "Toast and orange juice."

"I thought so. We'll get something at the hotel after we talk to Calvin O'Reilly."

Dana frowned but said nothing. Her awareness of Brian, gone while she talked about her business venture, reappeared full force. She didn't know why she felt so ambivalent about him, but she had a feeling it had to do with the magic of first love. And she didn't even want to think about that.

The houses and pastures rushed by her window as Dana silently pondered her mixed feelings for Brian. Those mixed feelings dated back to that fateful day two years ago, the day of their college graduation. Dana was a young twenty-two, eager to get out on her own and conquer the world of merchandising. Brian was already twenty-seven; he'd been out in the world ever since he was eighteen. That was when his father died suddenly of a heart attack, halfway through Brian's first year of college. His hopes for a college degree and entrance into law school died with his father. He had to support his mother and his grandmother, two traditional homemaking women who'd had no experience in the workplace. And they were so deeply in mourning, one for her beloved husband, the other for her only son.

Looking back, Dana thought that Brian's obvious maturity was one of the first things that drew her to him. They had other things in common—music, a love of the islands and the outdoors—but he made her feel very feminine and beautiful. And she liked that; who wouldn't?

They'd dated for two years. Brian was proud that he was finally earning his degree, finishing up at the same time she did.

It was near the time of their graduation that Dana realized she was very much in love with Brian. He had already declared his love. It had scared her at first. She thought it was too soon; she was too young. But then she was caught up in the glow of new love and it was so wonderful . . .

But as graduation neared, Dana began to have doubts. Brian talked more and more of marriage and family. She knew she wasn't ready even though she did love him.

Then the night of the dance. It was wonderful. Exquisite. They had such a time!

A few days later it was graduation night. He had given her a beautiful pikake lei. After the ceremony she'd removed the other leis, taking off her black robe and wearing only the fragrant lei against her blue dress. They had stood together, he in the maile lei she had presented to him, receiving the congratulations of all their family and friends.

Dana saw the two Mrs. Vieiras exchanging

special looks but she hadn't a clue as to what would come. It wasn't until they were alone together that Brian dropped his bombshell.

Of course, *he* didn't think it was a bombshell. He was happy about it, hiding little smiles all evening. She'd thought it was because he planned to propose. And she was still agonizing over an answer. She wanted to marry him, but she still felt she was too young for a lifelong commitment. On the other hand, if he believed in long engagements . . .

Late that evening, after all the family celebrations, Dana and Brian sat on the bench in the Japanese pavilion at Liliuokalani Park. It was their favorite place and she felt sure Brian had brought her there to propose.

If only she'd known! But perhaps it wouldn't have made any difference.

They sat together holding hands, looking out at the moonlit bay.

"I've been wanting to tell you all night," Brian began.

Dana looked over at him and smiled. Here it was. He was going to tell her he loved her and then he would propose.

"I've found a wonderful job for you, Dana."

Dana couldn't believe it. Her mouth actually fell open in surprise. Brian didn't seem to notice. He went right on talking.

"My old high school buddy, Keanu Johansen, is with E.L.M.'s," he said, naming the most upscale department store on the island. "He says they can always use smart young women as managers and buyers. All you have to do is give him a call and the job is yours."

He was so proud of himself he squeezed her hand. Dana stared at him, still in shock. He claimed to love her and yet he was trying to run her life like she was a young schoolgirl. He knew she already had the job she wanted all lined up and ready.

Dana pulled her hand away from his and stood. "Take me home right now, Brian."

She saw his look of surprise. It just added to her anger.

And all the way to her house he kept on asking her what was wrong, telling her he loved her.

When he finally pulled into her driveway she turned toward him. "Brian, if you don't understand why I'm upset then you don't know me at all. I *have* a job; I don't need you to line one up for me. I am perfectly capable of getting one on my own merits, and I did."

Despite her best efforts to control them, tears ran down her cheeks. "I thought I loved you but now I find I don't know you at all."

He tried to interrupt, to talk, but she just kept shaking her head.

"No, Brian, it's no good. This is it. I'm too young for marriage, and too old for a father. Good-bye."

And with those decisive words she did what she had regretted forever afterward. She yanked the lei from her shoulders and tossed it into his lap. That beautiful pikake lei, fragile and delicate, the flower so many brides chose, the symbol of love and esteem . . . And she'd tossed it carelessly into his lap.

Then she stormed out of the car and up the stairs. And out of his life.

When she came out of her turbulent dreams of the past, they were pulling into the long drive leading up to the Mauna Kea Beach Hotel. She'd daydreamed her way through the end of the trip.

Chapter Three

Dana loved the Mauna Kea Beach Hotel. Opened thirty years ago by Laurance Rockefeller, it was the first of the grand hotels along the northwest coast of the Big Island. It was considered old now, but she loved the graceful white building, the beautiful golf course and gardens, and most of all, the pristine white sand beach that stretched out beyond it.

As they walked into the wide open-air lobby, her anxiety about her father, temporarily forgotten during the long ride with its enforced contact with Brian, reappeared. Once again Dana remembered the purpose of this visit, and the importance of speaking to Calvin O'Reilly.

Dana tried to conceal her impatience as Brian spoke to the woman at the desk. But after their first few words, she found herself heading back out to the front entrance, peering toward the lush green fairways just visible across the drive. Her father could be out there right now, enjoying a game of golf with an old friend. She prayed that he was. She didn't want to consider what might be happening if he wasn't.

Dana was frowning at the sun-splashed landscape when Brian approached, smiling his most reassuring smile. "He's still out on the golf course. Why don't we go over to the ninteenth hole for some lunch, and we'll be right there when they come in."

As Brian started across the entry, Dana seemed to come out of a trance and began to follow him, then stopped.

"Brian. Wait. I have to call the house and play back my messages." She fumbled in her purse for the remote that activated the machine. "Just in case," she added.

But the small hope was futile. Although there were several messages, all were from friends of Ike calling to see if he was back yet.

Brian remained silent as they walked along the path connecting the main building with the pro shop and restaurant. The trade winds drifted through the palm trees lining the drive, causing them to bend and sway, dancing their own graceful hula to the music of the rustling fronds. The sky was a clear azure, the grass of the golf course a rich green. Was it Dana's presence or the bright midday sun? Everything seemed more intense: the colors, the sounds of tree and surf, the scents of newly cut grass and tropical blossoms. He hoped that the calm and the beauty of the setting would pull Dana out of her funk the way the ride over had.

A quick look at Dana indicated it was not to be. Gloom settled around her like one of Hilo's inevitable rain clouds, shielding her from the warmth of the Kohala Coast's eternal sun. His inability to make things better for her tore at his heart. And the familiar pain irritated him.

Why did this woman in particular have such an effect on him? He'd asked himself that question many times over the years, and had yet to come up with an entirely satisfactory answer.

Brian glanced over at Dana. She was certainly attractive. Those beautiful dark eyes, usually sparkling with life, but currently clouded with anxiety over her father. Her little snip of a nose, the slight jut of her chin. Those wonderful sensuous lips . . .

Brian pulled his roving mind back in line. Many other women were equally attractive, or even more so. As he watched her, Dana straightened her back, pulling her head up higher and setting her shoulders back. With that small action, the worry in her eyes changed to determination.

Brian's lips turned up in a private smile. She might be vulnerable, but she could stand up to pressure and not let it pull her down. He'd never seen her in such a situation before, and if he'd considered it, he would have pictured Dana collapsing in tears and letting him comfort her. He'd never seen that inner strength, but he was impressed by it.

Not a word was spoken until they reached the restaurant. Brian found a table, then went into the pro shop to tell them where he could be found when the twosome returned.

Dana stared at the menu, her eyes on the printed words but her mind focused inward.

Brian made small talk for a few minutes, talking about the golf pro, who'd turned out to be a former schoolmate. Dana listened with half a mind, the other half busy convincing herself that her dad would be all right. Finally she pulled herself together, telling herself that she would be useless to her father if she fell apart from either depression or hunger.

Spearing a piece of turkey from her chef's salad with her fork, she put it in her mouth and chewed. Surprisingly, it tasted delicious. She'd expected everything to taste like sawdust—to match her mood, perhaps.

A short silence had fallen and held from the time the waitress appeared with their food. Now Dana looked over at Brian thoughtfully.

"In the car, we talked about my dreams becoming reality." Her dark eyes peered into his lighter ones, trying to read something there. "What about your dreams, Brian? Are you still involved with politics?"

Brian smiled. "I'm still active in the party, yes. I hope to run for the council next election. I've been building up my following in the party these last two years."

Dana remembered long pleasant afternoons sitting on a mat at the beach or their favorite place, Liliuokalani Park, just lounging and talking over their future plans. Of course those memories were bittersweet, because although she tried to encourage Brian's political aspirations, he always seemed ready to discourage her dreams of a small shop. Maybe discourage was the wrong word—maybe it was just that he kept trying to push her in other directions.

Well, this wasn't the time to resurrect old aches.

"Will it be a problem that you're still a bachelor?"

Brian frowned at her. He hoped she didn't

think the only reason he'd wanted a family was to further his political ambitions.

"I don't think so, but it's hard to predict what the voters will do. Anyway, I hope to get elected on the issues, and my stands on them, not my personal life-style."

Dana smiled. Could he be that naive? Not in real life certainly, but maybe on this one issue.

Looking down, she noted with surprise that she'd eaten almost half of her salad. Brian was starting the second half of his club sandwich.

"How are your mother and Vovo?"

When Brian moved back into his parents' house after his father's death, he'd thought it would be temporary. But somehow the timing had never seemed right for him to get his own place, and he still lived at home with his mother and grandmother.

"They're both fine." He smiled across the table, a hint of mischief in the grin. "They keep me well informed of all your activities."

Dana blushed. She'd loved the two friendly women. It had hurt almost as much losing them as it had losing Brian.

"I was thinking of calling them. Do they still crochet and embroider?"

At Brian's affirmative reply she went on to explain that she might have a small gift counter at her store, possibly with some items that would be appropriate for a bride. She thought some of the lovely crochet and embroidery the ladies made would be a nice addition. "I'd like to have a ring bearer's pillow made up—I have an idea for the design. I'll have to call them."

"I'm sure they'll enjoy hearing from you." Brian had to smile. It would enable them to pump the source for information—like how she might feel about a certain former boyfriend. Yes, he wouldn't mind in the least if she talked to his mother and Vovo.

He had finished his sandwich and Dana was picking over the remains of her salad, when the golf pro approached their table.

"That twosome you're waiting for just pulled into the garage. If you go out back now, you should be able to catch them."

By the time Brian rose from his chair and turned toward the golf course exit, Dana was already out the door. He managed to catch up with her just as two men appeared from the cart garage.

Brian heard Dana's sigh of disappointment as she caught sight of them. Both were haoles, one tall, trim, and tanned, the other about as tall as Brian's five-eleven, but portly and very fair. His face and his arms below the short sleeves of his golf shirt were a bright red.

"Mr. O'Reilly?" Dana asked, putting her hand out.

It was the sunburned man who took it, greeting her with a huge grin.

"Now that's what I call a real nice reception, Tom," he said, turning toward his golf buddy. The broad vowels and his down-home manner bespoke a Texas background.

"I'll say. Some people have all the luck."

Brian stepped forward and introduced himself and Dana, inviting the two men to come inside and share some iced tea. Tom excused himself after hearing the nature of the matter, and the three made themselves comfortable back at the table.

Brian retold the story, with help now and again from Dana. Cal was visibly affected by the tale.

"I sure do wish I could help you, but I'm as lost as you are." His bright blue eyes were clouded with concern as he looked from Dana to Brian and back again.

Dana urged him to tell them whatever he could about his contact with her father.

"Well, now, I wrote Ike a letter saying I would be here. Got in late Tuesday, so I didn't call till Wednesday morning. We were going to meet for dinner last night. But Ike said he doesn't like to drive much at night anymore. So we decided we would meet for lunch." Cal paused long enough to take a long sip of his tea, then shook his head. "But he didn't turn up. I called his house a time or two, but all I got was a busy signal."

"Oh, dear," Dana mumbled. "That was me, calling around, trying to see if anyone knew where he was. We didn't find out about you until this morning."

"I'd sure like to help if I can."

Cal's voice was sincere, but Brian shook his head. "Just call us if you hear from him. And thanks."

Dana felt deflated. She'd put so much hope in her theory that Ike was the unknown guest golfer. The atmosphere in the car as they started back was heavy once more.

As they neared the town of Kamuela, Dana sat up straighter and peered out the window. A light rain had begun, actually little more than a mist, but it was enough to cloud the windshield and inhibit her view. She leaned forward, peering through the damp windshield.

"Brian, pull over. Here, on this next road." She pointed to a narrow road off to the right. Her voice was excited and she talked fast, as though she had to say it all before they passed by the upcoming turn.

"Brian, I just remembered. We used to come

out here all the time to visit my mom's Aunty Lillian. She lived right down here somewhere. The way Dad's been lately, if he was passing through here, he may have stopped to see her, even though she's been dead for years. Anyway, it's worth a stop, as long as we're out here, don't you think?"

Brian's brows came together as he glanced at Dana and instantly culled the most pertinent bit of information from her urgent chatter. He turned onto the road she indicated, then pulled off onto the shoulder and stopped. He shifted in the seat until he could look directly at her.

"What do you mean, 'the way Dad's been lately'?"

The look he gave her was one she felt sure he must use to spear alleged criminals during interrogations. She squirmed uncomfortably beneath it, the way she imagined the suspects did.

"Nothing," she began, wetting her lips with the tip of her tongue.

Brian refused to be distracted. He kept his eyes on hers, waiting.

"Nothing particular. I told you . . . he hasn't been himself."

Brian continued to watch her. "Okay, Dana. I think it's time I heard about the woman's intuition you mentioned yesterday—the forgetfulness, whatever. I have a feeling you aren't leveling with me and I want to know why. What is there you haven't told me?"

Dana swallowed hard. She'd known this moment would come, of course, but she'd hoped Ike would turn up before it became necessary. She should have realized Brian was too smart not to figure it out so quickly.

Dana couldn't meet his eyes. "Like I told you yesterday, mostly it's just little things. By themselves they don't really mean anything. It's just since he disappeared that I've been putting things together, and the picture I get is really making me worry."

With as few words as possible, Dana proceeded to tell Brian about Ike's short memory lapses, and the condition of the yard and house.

"And just last week I got a call from Mr. Kanoa."

Brian nodded. Thirty years ago, the Kanoas and Longs built their homes on adjacent lots, and they had been good friends and neighbors ever since.

"Mr. Kanoa found Ike wandering in his backyard. He said he looked confused. But the reason he called me was that Ike asked him if he'd seen Rose."

Brian raised his eyebrows. "No wonder you're

worried." Brian also knew that Rose Long had been dead for eight years.

"I went over straight after work. It was only an hour or so later, and Dad was his usual self. It was five o'clock and he was sitting down to dinner right on schedule. I tried to ask him about going over next door, but he couldn't seem to remember anything about it."

She stared into Brian's eyes for a moment. "I didn't want to publicize the search as one for a confused old man who'd wandered off and gotten lost. I couldn't do that to Dad."

Brian took her hand, running his fingers over her wrist in a soothing motion. She'd stopped short of admitting her guilt for not recognizing earlier that something was so wrong; but of course Brian recognized that too.

"You can't blame yourself, Dana. You admitted that most of these were isolated incidents that don't mean a thing. But I agree with you. Put them all together and it's a different situation."

Trying to remove the blame from Dana's shoulders, he put it on his own, cursing himself for the emotional involvement that made him forget that the subject's health was an important factor in investigating a missing person case.

"But you can't tell everyone, Brian." Dana's

eyes pleaded with him. "How could he ever live it down if we tell the world he's a confused old man who's gotten lost?"

"Dana." Brian reached over and ran his fingers lightly down her cheek. He hoped the light touch was reassuring, as he meant it to be. At least for her. For himself, the touch burned, and his heartbeat accelerated. With an effort, he kept his voice soft and calming. "Do you think I would purposely do anything to embarrass your dad?"

Dana stared into his eyes. The pupils had widened, so his eyes looked much darker than usual and they sparkled with—it must be affection. The light touch of his fingers still resting against her jawline was doing funny things to her thinking processes, but she did know that Brian would never willingly hurt her father. That he liked and respected Ike was never in doubt. "No."

With a sigh of relief, Brian put the car into drive. "Show me the way."

Dana found the turnoff with an ease that surprised her. It had been a long time since she'd been out here and there had been a lot of building in this area recently. The old pastureland was rapidly becoming subdivisions.

And then she saw it—just ahead, a big old house set in a picturesque field, a running brook nearby, foothills in the distance. The roof was brown instead of red, but it was remarkably the same as she remembered, from the graveled driveway to the blue-white hydrangeas blooming along the front of the wide porch.

"Hello!" Dana called a greeting to the unfamiliar woman who came out onto the porch at the sound of their car. "Does the Lucas family still live here?"

The woman, a few years older than Dana and several months into a pregnancy, replied in the affirmative, and Dana introduced herself as a cousin from Hilo.

With an old-fashioned, country-style aloha, the woman introduced herself as Pam and invited them inside, urging them to sit while she got some refreshments and called her husband, Dana's cousin Rusty.

Leaving them alone in the living room for a few minutes, she returned with tall glasses of punch and a plate of home-baked cookies. Pam chattered away, obviously delighted to have some company.

"Rusty will be right in. He's fixing up the old pigpen for the dog. She had eleven puppies under the house—can you believe it? Now that they're starting to move around they need a safer place.

"Oh, Rusty, there you are. Do you remember your cousin Dana from Hilo?"

"Hey, cuz." Rusty greeted Dana with a big bear hug. "I remember how you used to tag along with me everywhere." He winked at Brian. "A real pest she was."

Brian laughed, Dana looked embarrassed, and Pam saved the moment by asking if they were just passing through.

So Dana began to recite the story once again, explaining about her father disappearing, apparently on his way to the Mauna Kea Beach Hotel. Instead of calling him confused, Dana said he seemed to be reliving some of his past, and she'd suddenly remembered the visits to great-aunt Lillian.

Rusty and Pam said they were sorry to hear about Ike, assured them they would call if they heard anything, and waved them off with urgings to come again.

The long drive back to Hilo was quiet. Both Brian and Dana were reviewing the day's events, deciding what helped and what didn't.

Dana stirred restlessly in the stuffy car, finally opening her window despite the misty rain that continued to fall outside. The fresh air was revitalizing and definitely necessary, even if it meant getting a little damp.

She said silent prayers as her eyes roved the

landscape, glancing over the rolling mountain foothills, across green pastures and close-cut lawns. Unconsciously she noted any people, especially men, and most especially older men. Would she find him this way, through dumb luck and mere chance.

Dana looked straight ahead as they rounded a curve. And drew in her breath in awe. Ahead of them the roadway ran up a small hill. But it was the sight of the horizon beyond that had Dana mesmerized.

An eerie pink and gold light seemed to radiate into the sky from behind that near hill. But before she could question Brian about the strange phenomenon, they'd crested the hill and found the cause.

Even in this land of rainbows, Dana had never seen anything quite like this. For it was a rainbow that caused that eerie glow—a rainbow that lay across the rain-damp landscape like a long, sheer ribbon.

"Oh, my." It was barely a whisper, just a breath of sound, as she stared at the beautiful sight, afraid to look away in case it disappeared.

"Wow." Brian too was affected by the unusual rainbow.

Then the intensity of the rain shower increased, washing away the beautiful vision, and it was gone as quickly as it had come.

Brian shook his head. "I've never seen a rainbow that low before."

"It's a sign." Dana looked over to Brian, a serene look in her eyes, a trace of a smile on her lips. "I've been working hard to find Dad, Brian, but most of all I've been praying. Don't you think that could be a sign that all will be well? It's what the rainbow meant, isn't it? That all would be well after the floods; that it would never happen again."

Brian kept his eyes on the road. How could he answer that? They were driving through the town of Kamuela now and there was more traffic, a good excuse not to look over at Dana. He didn't want to discourage her, and he did have strong faith . . . but he wasn't at all sure that such wondrous signs appeared to individuals in this day and age.

But apparently Dana didn't need any agreement from him. She reached over, flipped on the radio, and turned introspective once more.

Chapter Four

Brian woke early the next morning after a restless night. Seeing Dana again had brought so many bittersweet memories. They haunted his dreams—and his waking hours as well.

With Dana so much on his mind, he picked up the phone to check in with her. He muttered under his breath when he got the answering machine. The thought of speaking to Dana first thing in the morning had a definite appeal.

She must be in the shower, he decided, heading that way himself.

But when he got out of the shower, dressed, and still got only the answering machine, he began to worry.

"Who you calling so early on Sunday?" Brian's mother took the pan of scrambled eggs off the stove and stared at him as he dialed yet again.

"It's his day off, Geraldine," Brian's grandmother answered for him. "Setting up a big date, Brian?"

"How can he be going on a big date when Dana's father is missing?" Brian's mother leaned over the table to fill the plates with the eggs, then went back to the counter for the bacon and toast.

"Well, he's probably working on that right now, aren't you, Brian?"

Used to his relatives providing his answers for him, Brian waited to see if it was his turn to speak. When both women looked over at him expectantly, he answered. "I've been trying to check in with Dana for the past hour but all I get is her answering machine. I'm beginning to wonder where she could be."

Geraldine and her mother-in-law exchanged a significant look.

"We know where she is."

"You mean we know where she *probably* is."

Brian put down his fork and stared at the two women. He loved them dearly but they could be extremely frustrating. "Where?"

Geraldine finished chewing her toast and wiped the side of her mouth with her napkin.

"Last night after church she mentioned she was going to paint her store."

"If I'm worried, I like to get out and do something like painting or gardening or something," Bernice said.

Brian had to smile. That at least was true. His seventy-eight-year-old grandmother Bernice, whom he'd called Vovo since he was a child, liked nothing more than getting "down and dirty," whether it was doing housework, yardwork, or general repairs. The excellent condition of the old house was largely due to her efforts.

Brian rushed through the rest of his breakfast, much to the consternation of the women. Now that he knew where to look for Dana, he could hardly wait to start.

"You shouldn't eat so fast, dear."

"Yeah, I know. But I've got to go. I'll be working." And he was out the door.

Geraldine and Bernice exchanged smiles.

"We may have a wedding after all," Geraldine said softly. It wouldn't do to have Brian overhear.

Bernice moved her head slowly back and forth. "Two years late. What a waste."

Dana was indeed painting the store. She was dressed in old frayed shorts and faded T-shirt, with paint spatters large and small covering all parts of her body. Brian thought she looked beautiful.

"You should have covered your hair."

Dana jumped, splashing more paint on her already bespeckled arms. "Brian! You startled me.

"What are you—?" she began, before turning suddenly, almost hitting Brian in the face with the wet pink roller. Her face was tense with suppressed emotion. "Did you find him?"

"No." Brian ran his fingers through his hair. His eyes mirrored his regret. "Gee, Dana, I'm sorry. I just came over to see how you were doing."

"Oh." Dana put the roller into the pan and walked back to the small restroom to wash her hands.

Brian followed. "I was worried when I couldn't get hold of you this morning. Mom and Vovo thought you might be here."

Dana smiled, but she seemed skeptical. "You were worried?"

Brian reached around her to dampen some paper towels, then applied them to the paint on her face. His hands were gentle, his eyes tender. Within moments, Dana was lost amid a whirlpool of feelings. Her eyes searched his face as he concentrated on removing the paint. She began to feel very warm.

When the paint was gone and Brian continued to hold on to her chin, she stayed immobile. When his head began to lower, her lips parted ever so slightly.

It was all the invitation he needed. Brian set his lips against hers, gently, almost tentatively. She was warm and smooth and so sweet. He'd never forgotten the feel and the taste of Dana's lips and it was just as he'd remembered.

His hand moved from her chin into her hair, his rough fingers rubbing through the fine strands and massaging her scalp. Dana sighed against him, and his other hand went around to her back, bringing her soft body up against him. She fit perfectly against him; they complimented each other so well.

As he continued to deepen the kiss, Brian could feel Dana responding. Her arms moved up around his neck, one hand tangling in his thick hair. She pressed her body more firmly against him, and then he realized he had to stop—or never stop at all. And though he hated to move away, he knew it was too soon for this.

With great reluctance he ended the kiss, released Dana, and took a step back. He stared at her half-closed eyes and kiss-swollen lips and wanted to pull her back into his arms for more of the same. Instead, he ran his hand through his hair, rearranging the dark waves across his forehead. And turned away.

Dana observed his withdrawal. Unable to watch any longer as he continued to turn away from her, she moved back to the sink and began to scrub at the paint on her arms. What on earth was she doing, falling back into his arms like some lovesick teenager!

She scrubbed until her arms were pink, then turned off the water. She didn't feel entirely ready to face Brian, so she took more dampened paper towels and began to scrub at the paint on her legs. It gave her a little more time and space.

Finally, she moved into the next room, surprised to find Brian finishing up the wall she'd been painting when he entered, the last bit to be done. But, no, she reminded herself. She shouldn't be surprised. It was just Brian taking over like he always did. Next he'd be telling her what to do and how to do it. She straightened her back and set her lips. Let him try.

"This is a good color," Brian told her. He stepped back to admire the shell-pink wall he'd just finished. "Restful. What else are you going to do?"

Surprise robbed Dana of speech for a moment. This must be a new Brian—complimentary, and interested in what she was doing. But it was nice.

Tentatively at first, then with more assurance as she warmed to her topic, she described how she planned to divide the store into a large work area with a more intimate living-room atmosphere at the front of the store for customers. "The bridal party can come in and sit comfortably while we choose their designs. There'll be a screen to separate the workroom and fitting room," she added, throwing her arm out to indicate the large screen at the back of the room, then waving her other hand to show him the area where it would be positioned.

Brian nodded. He helped her put away the paint supplies as she described the other incidentals. She was so excited about the store. She talked on about problems and considerations in choosing things like curtains and carpet and display mannequins.

Brian listened with interest to all her plans. He enjoyed watching Dana as she described everything she'd done and planned to do. He encouraged her to go on because she was more animated than he'd seen her in the last two days. This activity was just what she needed to get her mind off her major worry—Ike.

As she pulled the drop cloths from the furniture and worktables, she explained how she and her assistant Malia had made matching slipcovers for the assortment of upholstered furniture she'd accumulated for the front of the store. But it was the sight of her sewing machines and a pile of shimmering fabrics that gave him an idea that might help keep her distracted.

"Do you have a phone in here?"

Dana directed him to it, then busied herself, trying not to eavesdrop. Was he checking in with the police department about Ike? He would tell her if they learned anything, wouldn't he? But he kept his body turned away from her, and what little she heard didn't sound like it had any relation to the missing person case.

After the call, he approached her with a smile on his face. "Let's go. I want you to meet someone."

Dana frowned. "Who?"

Brian tried to look serious, but there was a smile lurking behind his eyes. "What is this? Can't I surprise you?"

Dana watched him through narrowed eyes. "It depends. This isn't about Ike, is it?"

The laughter was immediately gone. "No. I would tell you right away if he was found."

Dana believed him. She could see he was hurt that she'd felt the need to ask. But she was leery. She didn't know what to make of Brian right now. He seemed to move back and forth from the old authoritarian Brian to a new, gentler, more understanding Brian; she didn't know which was the true man.

"Come on, Dana, trust me. You'll like this."

Within minutes, she was seated in Brian's car, heading out of the downtown area. Mauna Kea loomed before them, blue-green against an azure sky. She enjoyed the ride, but when Brian pulled into the driveway of a beautiful, expensive home, Dana looked over at him in dismay.

"Brian Vieira! I'm an awful mess, in paint-stained clothes, and you bring me here—to this gorgeous house."

"Pualani won't mind. She's a casual person."

He got out of the car, walking around to meet Dana as she hesitated at her half-opened door. "She's a dispatcher at the station, and a great person." He held his hand out to Dana. "Come on."

Reluctantly, Dana took his hand and followed him to the door. But she wished she didn't look so bedraggled.

An attractive woman of about forty greeted them at the door and Dana was forced to wonder about Brian's definition of casual. Obviously, it was a male observation. For while their hostess wore shorts and a T-shirt, Dana recognized the matching set as an expensive designer item, available only at the best stores.

But Pualani was so friendly and welcoming, Dana quickly forgot her paint-spattered clothes.

Pualani led them through the house to a shady lanai, which also put Dana at ease—being outside didn't make her feel quite so out of place. She waved them toward a large glass-topped table where coffee and a basket of still-warm *malasadas* awaited them.

"So, did Brian tell you why you're here?" Pualani asked.

She laughed at Dana's confused expression. "Obviously not. That's okay, I'd like to explain myself. My husband is Sam Yoshiyama."

Dana recognized the name of the county attorney. Word had it that he planned to run for mayor, then eventually for governor. Pualani confirmed part of this with her next sentence.

"He's planning to run for mayor next year, so we go to all the important party functions. Anyway, the president is going to be in Honolulu next month on his way back from Japan, and there's going to be a big fund-raiser. Very formal."

She stopped talking to urge the basket of sweet donutlike confections on them. Dana was enjoying her coffee, but even the thought of the sugary *malasadas* made her stomach turn. Brian, however, helped himself.

"Sam told me to get something new, and I've been looking for a dress." She met Dana's eye in a woman-to-woman manner. "Have you ever looked for a nice formal dress in Hilo?"

Dana commiserated with her. That was why she hoped to do well in her own shop. "Next month at this time, I'll be able to recommend my shop, Lokelani's. But, as Brian can tell you, right now it's just a newly painted shell with a jumble of worktables and furniture in it."

"Yes, he did tell me." Pualani glanced over at Brian, passing him the basket of *malasadas* again. "Go ahead and finish them," she said, turning back to Dana. "We women have to watch our figures, more's the shame. Anyway, I was hoping I could talk you into opening up early. Brian suggested it, actually. It would really mean a lot to me, and if you're as good as Brian claims, it could bring more work your way."

Dana turned to Brian, her eyes confused, her jaw slack with surprise. "Brian recommended . . ." Her voice trailed off as she stared at his complacent grin.

Unaware of the subtle undercurrents passing between the couple, Pualani continued.

"Oh, Brian thinks you're the best seamstress on the island. He told everyone at work about your new store, and about the wonderful job you did on the dresses for your cousin Allison's wedding. So will you do it?"

Dana was still staring at Brian and almost missed the question. She had to shake herself internally to get back to business.

"Of course I'll do it. Did you say you need it in a month?"

"Is it too soon?"

"Oh no, it's not that. I don't have anything else I'm working on at the moment, but with my father missing and the store opening set . . ."

"Oh, I understand. And I'm so sorry. But actually I thought this might help keep your mind off your father. You know, something to keep your hands busy and your mind off the what-ifs."

Dana had to agree it seemed like a good idea. And with only the one item to do, a month was plenty of time. Brian finished off the pastries while the two women talked of basic styles and fabrics and made arrangements to get together. By the time everything had been set up, Dana and Pualani felt like old friends. And Pualani set her so much at ease, she completely forgot about her paint-stained clothes.

But all her initial confusion swept back through Dana as soon as she and Brian were alone in the car. She angled herself toward Brian so she could look at him during the short drive back to the store. "You think I'm the greatest seamstress on this island?"

Brian looked uncomfortable, but managed to shrug and reply casually. "You *are* a good seamstress, Dana."

"But you always fussed at me for wanting to sew. You went crazy when I said I was taking the job with Hawaiian Holiday Wear."

"I do not fuss."

Brian's voice was cool and steady, but she could tell he wasn't happy with her choice of words. She brought her hand up to muffle a giggle at the thought of the macho Brian fussing in the manner of Lucy Ricardo on those old sitcoms. It was an absurd picture.

"Okay," she admitted, "maybe you didn't fuss. But you did get after me about my choices."

Brian shrugged but kept his eyes on the road ahead. "I just thought you could do better. Hawaiian Holiday Wear worked you too hard and paid only minimum wage. You could have had a management position after four years of college."

He didn't say it, but Dana knew he was thinking of the job at E.L.M.'s.

Dana blew out a long breath, then straightened in her seat, facing forward once again. Some things never changed. No matter how many times she explained to Brian that she took that job for the experience, he had insisted that there was something better out there. If he'd listened, she would have explained that she'd taken that particular job only temporarily, planning to move on into management in six months' time. But he'd never grasped the fact that she also had her life planned out—not in the staid field he had picked for his, but in a more artistic endeavor. But nonetheless her life plan had validity, and she'd finally decided to pursue it without him.

Still, he'd recommended her for a lucrative commission; even better, one that would put her handiwork before the cream of Hawaiian society. It could generate some important commissions for her. She would never have thought she'd see him encourage her this way; he'd never seemed to approve of her career enough to do it. Yet he had.

As he pulled up beside her car in the lot across from the store, she turned toward him again, laying her hand on his right arm. Her voice was soft and utterly sincere. "Thank you, Brian, for the recommendation."

He put the car into park, leaning his left arm across the steering wheel so he could face her. "Anytime."

Then, before she could reach for the door handle, he bent his head and placed a light kiss on her lips.

Dana felt the gentle kiss all the way to her paint-spattered toes. Tiny beads of moisture formed along the top of her forehead and they had nothing to do with the seventy-eight degrees outside. Inside the car, the temperature was rising.

The look that passed between them was long. It smoldered with heat and emotion—and complications from the past.

Just before Dana gave in to impulse and pulled his lips back down to hers, she got control of herself, flung open the car door, and ran toward the empty store.

Brian stifled a curse when she failed to check for traffic as she ran across the street. Thank goodness it was Sunday and the only car in sight was traveling slowly, more than a block away. He considered going after her, but decided against it. Let her stew over her rediscovered feelings. Why shouldn't she be as unsettled as he was?

With a satisfied grin he backed the car from the parking slot.

The phone was ringing when Dana returned to the house. It seemed to be a constant in her life these past few days—the ring of the phone, the press of the receiver against her ear, busy signals and electronic beeps and recorded voices asking her to leave a message.

But she was still praying for some clue that would lead them to Ike, so she dropped the grocery bag she held and raced to the kitchen phone.

"Hello, Dana?"

It was a male voice, rough and throaty, vaguely familiar.

"It's Roy Gonsalves. I'm calling about Ike."

Dana felt a painful clenching in her chest that stopped her breath. She had to suck in some air before she could ask the important question of her father's old friend.

"Have you seen him?"

"Well . . ." He paused to clear his throat, then coughed a few times before continuing. "I was at the airport yesterday. My daughter was leaving for Honolulu."

Dana sighed quietly. It took more patience than she had these days to listen to Ike's friends ramble once they got her on the phone.

As he began to explain why his daughter was on her way to Honolulu, Dana was compelled to interrupt.

"Mr. Gonsalves." She felt bad cutting him off this way, but if he'd seen Ike she really needed to know. Immediately. "Did you say you saw my dad?"

He coughed again before replying. "Well, I saw someone who looked a lot like him."

He paused once again to clear his throat and Dana clenched her fingers around the receiver until they were white. *Please, please, get on with it*, she pleaded silently.

"The Maui flight was just boarding when we got inside. I saw this guy going through the gate there. He looked a lot like Ike. I tried to call after him, but he was already through the glass doors. Then this morning I find out Ike's missing. So I figure I let you know; you must know where he would go if he's on Maui."

So that explained why he hadn't phoned yesterday.

As she thanked him for calling, Dana felt a burgeoning excitement within her at this new clue. "Thanks again for calling, Mr. Gonsalves. This could be just the break we need."

Dana hung up, deep in thought. She had never considered the chance that her father might have gone off the island. It brought out numerous possibilities. Ike had many friends and relatives on the other islands. Though it still didn't answer the question of why he would disappear for—what was it now since he'd last been seen, four days?—without calling to tell her.

She considered her next course of action while she rescued the abandoned grocery bag and put the perishables away. First of all, she had to call Brian.

Minutes later she hung up the phone and deliberated her next move. Brian was not at the station and not at home, though she left messages at both places. Dana told herself that Brian was a busy police detective and this was, after all, a low-priority case. Although a seventy-year-old man was missing, there was no evidence of foul play, or any indication that he was in danger. So it was up to her to pursue this lead.

Dana organized herself at the kitchen table with her father's address book and began the time-consuming task of calling everyone in it. She started with Maui.

Dana had just hung up the phone when a brisk knock called her to the front door. Not unexpectedly, she found Brian standing there.

"Dana," he began. Then he took a closer look

at her shining eyes and relaxed expression. "I've been calling for an hour and all I get is a busy signal. What have you learned that you haven't told me?"

Dana straightened her back and met his gaze. "I called you as soon as I heard." Then she broke into a grin as she led him into the kitchen. "Come in here where I have all my notes. I have to start at the beginning."

She proceeded to tell him about Mr. Gonsalves' trip to the airport and what he had reported, going on to explain about the address book and her phone calls.

Brian wasn't surprised this time. However, he was exasperated with her. "If you had told someone at the station about that initial call, we could have checked with the airlines for a passenger list."

"Oh. I didn't think of that." Dana was momentarily nonplussed.

But only momentarily. "But I haven't gotten to the best part yet. I called all the Maui numbers in Dad's address book." Her long fingers smoothed out a page in the small book lying open on the kitchen table. "There's a listing for a Moses Palikapu. I remember Dad talking about him, though I haven't seen him since I was little. He's some kind of distant relative. Anyway, only his wife Jane was at home. She says Moki drove over to Hana for a few days— for a cousin's funeral. She didn't go because she hurt her back and she couldn't handle the long ride. And, Brian"—Dana was so excited she could hardly sit still—"he took several other people with him. She's not sure who, just that they were all relatives of some sort. And she was sure one of the men had flown over from Hilo." Dana leaned back in her chair, happy to think she had found this hopeful information on her own. "She said she'll try to track down Moki and find out who all is there with him."

Dana finished with a big smile, immensely proud of herself.

Brian hated to burst her bubble, but he saw a load of flaws in this new theory. She did look so pleased with herself though.

He decided to let her go on expecting the best. It might help her get a good night's sleep for a change.

He covered her hand, still lying over her notes on the table, with his. Her hand felt so tiny in his as he turned it over and clasped it snuggly, giving it a squeeze.

"Good work, Dana. And meanwhile I'll check with the airlines."

He kept hold of her hand while they rose to their feet and edged around the table. Brian looked down into her radiant face and couldn't resist. His lips covered hers, savoring her own unique honeyed taste, feeling the exquisite satin of her lips.

Dana's arms moved around his neck as she responded to his kiss. She felt so good, tasted so sweet . . .

Brian ended the kiss and moved away from Dana. He ran his fingers through his hair, pushing an unruly wave away from his forehead.

"Well." He started toward the door. "I'd better get going."

Dana followed slowly. She was probably wondering why he was such an idiot he didn't steal another kiss. But just as he hadn't wanted to take advantage when she was lost and defenseless with grief, so he didn't want to do it now when she was vulnerable with relief. Especially since he knew, even if she didn't, just how flimsy this new hope was.

Brian realized she was pinning her hopes on Ike's having gone to Maui for the funeral of a distant relative. It was the kind of thing Ike would do. But Brian had already thought of checking with the airlines, and none had reported Ike listed among their passengers during the last four days. Now of course he would check again, both with Roy Gonsalves and with Hawaiian and Aloha Airlines. Once he could pinpoint the exact flight, he could also show Ike's picture to flight attendants and ground crews in both Hilo and Kahului who might have seen him. He'd have to check Ike's credit card records too. If he *had* flown to Maui, he'd had to pay for the ticket somehow.

At the door he stopped and turned to Dana. Hope had infused her spirits, making her look more like the old Dana. What the heck. Another kiss couldn't hurt.

He gathered her into his arms and looked into her eyes, once again bright with hope. "Try to get some sleep tonight. Maybe you can get rid of these." He trailed one finger gently across her cheeks under her eyes where dark circles of fatigue showed.

Dana smiled. It was a real smile tonight too, not those half-hearted attempts she'd been offering lately. "Yes, doctor," she teased.

Brian smiled back. Then he pulled her close and dropped a whisper of a kiss on her lips. Just a little something to remember him by, he thought as he stepped down the stairs to his car. But almost too much for him. He doubted he'd have a restful night with the memory of how she felt in his arms so close and her scent still tickling his nostrils.

Brian sighed as he turned the key in the ignition. He could still see Dana standing just inside the door, her body silhouetted by the living room light. He hoped Jane Palikapu called her back soon. He didn't want to be the one to break the bad news to her.

Chapter Five

Once again the phone was ringing when Dana returned to the house. After the most restful night she'd had in four days, she had spent the morning at the store with Pualani. She'd shown her the specialty fabrics she had in stock and discussed the type of design that might work for Pualani's special dress. Pualani was still with her, but they had developed enough rapport that Dana felt comfortable dashing into the kitchen to pick up the phone, leaving the older woman alone in the living room.

Dana picked up the phone just as the recorded message from the answering machine finished playing. *Please, please*, Dana prayed, *let it be the call I'm expecting.*

"Hello? Hello?" The voice at the other end was tentative, uncertain.

"Yes. Hello." Dana spoke too loudly, and lowered her voice before proceeding. "I'm here. Hello?"

"Oh, thank goodness." The soft-spoken person at the other end of the line sounded relieved. "I always feel funny talking to those machines."

"Well, I'm here now. Can I help you?" Dana didn't recognize the voice, but it wasn't Jane on Maui. It sounded like an elderly woman, but Ike had so many friends, there was no way she could keep track of them all.

"Is this Ike's daughter?"

"Yes. Yes, it is." Dana wanted to scream in frustration. Did this person have some information for her or not? But of course she had to remain polite, try to keep hold of her patience, and wait for the woman to get to whatever it was she had to say.

"Oh, it's so nice to talk to you finally. I feel I know you, after everything Ike has told me about you. He's so proud of you."

"Really." Dana felt like an idiot as she gave another short reply. But what could she say?

"Oh, just listen to me rattle on. I called to tell you I think I saw Ike yesterday."

Dana pulled in her breath so quickly, a funny

squeak came out of her throat. She lowered herself into one of the kitchen chairs. "You did? What island are you calling from?"

The woman at the other end seemed surprised at this question. "Why, I'm right here in Hilo."

When Dana didn't say anything more she continued. "I'm not real sure it was him, you understand. Yesterday, that is. But I often see him in the hobby store, and we talk about our stamp collections."

Dana tried to breathe slowly and steadily as she silently urged the woman to go on. She was probably a lonely, neglected mother or grandmother and eager to talk to someone, anyone. Ike attracted people like that; he was so friendly and he enjoyed visiting with people so much.

But right now Dana just didn't have the time for this! She still hadn't heard from Jane Palikapu so she had to keep an open mind; much as she hoped that her father was attending a funeral on Maui, she had to acknowledge the possibility that he might not be there at all. And that meant that this woman, vague though she was, might have seen Ike on the Big Island yesterday.

The woman on the phone was continuing with her story. "My son picked me up yesterday. He took me out to his place for the night. He does it once a month and I stay over and go to church with them and have Sunday dinner." Her pride in this activity was evident in her voice.

"Where does he live?" Dana asked. She swore that once this was all over, she would call this woman back and let her talk as long as she wanted to, but right now she had to get her to tell her what she knew.

"Oh, didn't I say? He lives in Waikoloa Village. He has a good job with the Mauna Lani Resort. He's an electrician—"

Dana felt she had to interrupt or the conversation might last the rest of the afternoon. "Where did you see my dad, Mrs. . . . ?"

Good grief, all that talk and the woman had never even introduced herself.

"Mrs. Ho. You know, like Don Ho." A soft laugh traveled up the line. "No relation though."

Dana sighed. Mrs. Ho just couldn't stay on the subject. But Waikoloa Village was fairly close to the Mauna Kea Beach Hotel, the last place they knew for certain Ike was headed. How to get her back to the point?

"Mrs. Ho, you say you saw someone who looked like my dad?"

"Oh, dear, yes. I'm sorry, I do tend to go on.

You see, Dennis, that's my son, always stops at this little store on our way back to Hilo. It's right there on the main road through Kamuela—that newer shopping area across the street from the old Parker Ranch Center."

She was rambling again, but Dana let her go on. She knew the shopping center she meant. Now if only she would pinpoint the store.

"It's a hardware store, actually, run by this nice haole man, Johnson his name is. And he has just a few stamps and coins, but they're very nice. So Dennis always stops so I can go in and have a look. And just as we were leaving, I saw this gentleman down near the grocery store. I just saw him from behind, but it looked just like your dad. He was wearing a dark blue print aloha shirt too just like the report on the 'Mynah Bird' show said. I told Dennis to try to turn that way so that I could get a better look, but by the time we did he had disappeared."

"Thank you, Mrs. Ho. I really appreciate you calling me this way." It wasn't much but Dana was grateful for any lead. If he wasn't on Maui . . .

"Oh, do you really think this will help?" Mrs. Ho sounded so happy, Dana felt bad about her own impatience over the woman's plodding delivery.

"Yes, it might be just the clue we need," Dana

lied shamelessly. At least someone would be happy. But the vagueness of Mrs. Ho's story didn't give Dana a lot of hope. Of course, Roy Gonsalves' story hadn't been much better and that had led to her most encouraging news so far. Dana realized that if she hadn't placed all her dreams on finding Ike on Maui she would have been much more excited about Mrs. Ho's news. So she tried to be especially courteous. "If you give me your phone number, I'll be sure and let you know what happens."

Mrs. Ho was pathetically grateful for this consideration, and Dana made a careful note of her name and phone number so she could be sure to call her later.

"Good news?" Pualani asked. She was standing in the kitchen doorway watching Dana.

"Maybe." Dana had told Pualani of her hope that Ike would turn up visiting at a funeral in Hana, Maui. "That wasn't the woman on Maui." Dana sighed with frustration at having to wait to hear from her distant relatives on Maui. "But this Mrs. Ho thinks she saw him yesterday in Kamuela, in the area near the Parker Ranch Center."

Dana gestured toward the refrigerator. "Come on in here and help yourself to a soft drink while I try to call Brian."

Pualani took a can of guava juice from the

refrigerator and joined her at the kitchen table. Dana was on the phone for only a minute.

"He's out investigating a robbery, somewhere off Komohana."

Dana paced back and forth once, then stopped beside her newest client. "If you don't mind, could we do the measurements later? I've got to go out to Waimea."

Her pleading voice touched Pualani's soft heart. She assured Dana that they could get together again later. "But do you really think you should go out there alone?" Even though she was just a dispatcher, Pualani had been with the police department long enough to expect the worst.

Her concern made Dana think, and when she did leave, she was sitting in the passenger seat of Pualani's sea-green Oldsmobile.

Dana and Pualani left the last of the shops in the Parker Ranch Center, their flyers gone, Dana's hopeful heart once again low. They'd started across the highway at the grocery store Mrs. Ho had mentioned, covering all the stores there before driving over to this smaller, older shopping center. They'd stopped in every store, given everyone the flyer with the photo of Ike Long. No one recalled seeing a man of his description.

Dana was dragging her feet as they returned to the car, trying to remember that her best lead had yet to return her call. They had just stepped off the sidewalk when Dana saw Brian striding toward them. And she recognized the lowered brows, the pinched mouth, that tightness across his shoulders. He was angry.

"Why did you come out here alone?" He looked straight into Dana's eyes, ignoring Pualani completely.

Dana held her ground. He wouldn't intimidate her now. Ike was her father. She had every right to follow up a lead like this. There was no danger involved.

"I guess you got the message I left at the station."

Pualani stepped closer to Brian, her dark eyes examining his face with interest. "Hello, Brian."

Brian turned, apparently noticing her for the first time. He nodded a greeting before concentrating on Dana once more. "You should have waited for me."

"Honestly, Brian. Don't you think it's time you stopped treating me like a two-year-old? We agreed some time ago that this wasn't a kidnapping. I can certainly come out here and ask a few questions without being in any danger or creating difficulties for an investigation—or anything else that might cause trouble." Dana stopped long enough to pull in a deep breath. "So what's your problem?"

Brian ran his fingers through his hair, spreading the wavy strands in all directions. What *was* his problem? But he knew the answer. He just wanted to protect her from hurt. What if she'd found Ike out here? He might have been ill and disoriented, maybe even unconscious from a heart attack or worse. How would she have coped? Pualani at least should have known better.

Then again, he thought as he noted the firm set of Dana's chin, maybe she would have done just fine. Maybe *that* was what he was afraid of: that she didn't need him at all.

His fingers swept back through his hair, restoring it to some semblance of order. "I'm sorry, Dana. I was worried." He offered his hand. "Forgiven?"

Dana smiled. "Forgiven."

They shook on it, Brian holding on to her hand long after the handshake was over. Dana didn't seem to mind.

Standing beside them, completely forgotten, Pualani cleared her throat. "If it's all right with you two, I've got to get back to Hilo. Sam will wonder where I am if I'm not back by dinnertime."

With a quick wave, she moved off toward her car, leaving the younger couple looking embarrassed on the sidewalk. They'd completely forgotten about her.

On the long drive back to Hilo, Dana explained in detail the phone call that had sent her rushing off to Waimea again.

"I couldn't just leave this without checking it out, Brian. Jane still hasn't called from Maui. I don't understand what's taking so long but I guess she just can't get ahold of them."

Dana was silent for a moment, her eyes staring out the window, though she didn't even notice the pretty little waterfall they passed. "The call from Mrs. Ho . . . Brian, it was so sad. She just rambled on. I got the impression she's a very lonely person."

Brian could hear the agitation in her voice, could sense the turmoil behind what she was saying. He tried to reassure her. "But don't you think that's why Ike befriended her? Ike's such a friendly guy, he'll go up and talk to anyone who looks lonely."

"I know. I thought the same thing. Yet I can't help wondering . . ." Dana turned in the seat so she could face Brian. "Oh, Brian . . . You don't think Dad was the same way, do you? Do you think he was so lonely himself he filled his time rambling on over the phone to strangers?"

In the close confines of the car, Brian could feel her hurt and fear. She was blaming herself again, thinking she'd missed something important that should have been obvious. He was quick to reassure her. "I think he was just being his old self, talking to everyone he met, learning all about them. That's what he likes to do, Dana. You know that. He's a people person. He was probably on the listening end while Mrs. Ho babbled on. And remember, to him, she wasn't a stranger."

Dana breathed a sigh of relief. That's what she wanted to believe. Hearing it expressed out loud somehow made it more credible.

As usual, the phone rang as soon as she stepped into the house. Dana dashed into the kitchen, picking it up midway through the second ring.

"Hello, Dana? This is Moki Palikapu on Maui."

Dana felt her heart lodge in her throat as she responded to him. She couldn't swallow, could hardly breathe. If Ike was there, why wasn't he calling himself?

"I just heard about your father, Dana. I'm real sorry, but he's not here. I haven't seen him for two years now. I tried to call when our cousin Stanley died, but I never could get through. The phone was busy all the time."

Dana didn't know how she managed to keep up her end of the conversation until he hung up. Her disappointment was so great she could taste it.

When he finally said good-bye, promising to keep an eye out for Ike, Dana replaced the receiver of the wall-mounted phone, leaned her back against the wall, and slid down until she was sitting on the floor.

She'd put such great hope into that quick sighting of Roy Gonsalves. And now to have two promising leads fail in the space of a few hours.

Suddenly, it was all too much. Ike's disappearance. The horrible guilt. Brian being so nice. All the phone calls and sympathic noises.

She pulled her knees up to her chest and rested her forehead against them, wrapping her arms tightly around her legs. Right there in the kitchen, underneath the telephone, Dana finally let herself cry.

Brian knocked several times but there was no response. Odd. Dana's car was in the carport and when he dropped her off he'd promised to return shortly with some Chinese takeout.

With some trepidation he tried the door and

found it unlocked. Easing the bag of food quietly down onto the porch, he inched the door open. Just today, he'd been investigating the latest in a series of robberies not too far from this area. The perpetrators were still at large; small-time teen thieves were the best guess. Ike's house didn't fit the profile of the houses the punks had been hitting but the present situation was definitely suspicious. And the thieves were getting braver. The homeowner had been present during the last robbery, though she hadn't seen or heard anything. But it meant they were changing their modus operandi.

Brian eased himself fully into the house, standing quietly to listen. A small sound caught his attention. It sounded like a kitten mewling and seemed to be coming from the kitchen.

Reaching under his shirt for the gun he wore in a holster at his back, Brian stepped forward, walking as quietly as he could on the old floorboards. If some young punks had Dana in there—

A cold chill crept up his back and he had to pause to take a deep breath before he reached the door. It wouldn't do to confront a suspect in a temper.

Then he swung around the corner and into the kitchen.

Chapter Six

Brian's heart melted. The gun he'd pointed forward went quickly back into its holster. Dana was alone in the kitchen, sitting huddled on the floor beneath the telephone, her head on her drawn-up knees, her whole body shaking with her muffled sobs.

He moved straight to her side, lifting her into his arms and cradling her head tenderly against his shoulder. His voice was urgent even as he tried to comfort her.

"What's wrong, Dana? Are you all right?"

She managed to mumble half-coherent answers to his questions while continuing to cry against his shirtfront. She spoke of the call from Moki Palikapu and the way each promising tidbit had crumbled to nothing.

Brian made soft, incomprehensible noises in her ear, soothing her body by running his large hand gently up and down her back. It hurt him to see her in such distress, especially when there was so little he could do to comfort her. If only he didn't feel so helpless.

When she finally seemed to have cried herself out, he took her by the shoulders and moved her away from him. Looking down at her tear-drenched face, his heart filled with tenderness for this spirited woman. "I'm really sorry, Dana. About Maui, I mean. But it's about time you let yourself cry. Don't you feel better?"

Dana pushed her hair out of her face and sniffed loudly. "Yes, I think I do," she said, adding a thank-you as he handed her a handful of tissues from the box on the kitchen counter. She must look a wreck. But she had to agree, she did feel better. Having been held so tenderly in Brian's arms for the past ten minutes hadn't hurt any either.

"Good. Then come on." He led the way into the other room and reached outside the door for the abandoned bag of food.

As Brian urged food on her, he tried to offer some further options in their pursuit of Ike. Dana needed some hope to cling to, especially now when everything seemed so bleak.

But the truth was, he was fresh out of options. The checks of airline passenger lists and credit card receipts had drawn nothing. All he could do was urge Dana to go back through her lists and address books and call everyone she may not have reached the first time.

Brian didn't stay long after they ate. He left Dana at her door with a soft but lingering kiss. As he started down the steps, he glanced quickly across the street, winking at Dana. He was glad to see a smile tilt her lips. He wondered if Naomi was watching, and what conclusions she was drawing.

Dana kept her mind and body constantly occupied for the next two days. She spent hours on the telephone calling all the islands, but no helpful news surfaced. She and Malia spent long, sweaty hours organizing Lokelani's. She spent her days working in Ike's yard and garden and her nights working on Pualani's dress.

Brian was still busy with the string of robberies off Komohana. The thieves had been very busy the last few days, so she hardly saw him. They did speak on the phone every day, a constant reminder of the daily calls she could no longer make to Ike.

The call came unexpectedly.

Late Wednesday afternoon, Dana returned to Ike's with a load of clothes and personal objects from her apartment. She'd decided that she'd be better off moving back into her old room. Ike had often encouraged her to do this, saying it would be an economical move, but Dana had clung stubbornly to her hard-won independence. And look where it had gotten her.

Once again, she heard ringing as she inserted her key in the lock. Even though most of the hundred or so calls she'd taken these past five days had been of little import, Dana rushed inside to grab the phone before the machine picked up the call. It might be news about Ike. Or it might be Brian, calling when he could spare the time.

Too late. When she left the house that morning she'd set the answering machine to pick up on the second ring. She must have missed hearing the first, because by the time she had the door open, the ringing had stopped. And by the time she reached the bedroom phone where the machine was, the message had run and someone was speaking.

Stunned, Dana stood immobile for a full ten seconds before reaching for the receiver. For there on the answering machine speaker was her father's voice.

"Rose? Rose, is that you?"

The voice was tentative, inquiring. Ike sounded old and tired, but there was no question in her mind that the voice she was hearing belonged to her dad.

With shaking fingers she gripped the receiver, lifting it to her ear. The wavery voice was still speaking.

"Rose, honey, I've been trying to find you. Are you all right?"

Dana's heart went out to him even as she cringed as he asked once again for his deceased wife. She took a deep breath, trying to think back. He thought the voice on the machine belonged to her mother. How did her mother talk to him? She fought to keep her voice steady as tears flooded her eyes.

"Ike, love, I'm right here at home."

"Rose, Rose, is that you?" He sounded so eager and so relieved, Dana felt sick.

"Ike, love, where are you? I'll meet you—"

He was already speaking, apparently not hearing her words. "I'm coming, Rose."

"Wait." Dana wanted to ask again where he was, but before she could say anything else, she heard the click of the receiver at the other end. He'd hung up.

Dana collapsed on the floor beside the bed, the receiver still clutched in her hand. Tears dampened her cheeks but she resolutely blinked them back.

What had happened to her father? Sure, he

was old. Her parents had tried for so long to have a baby; as a child she had grown used to explaining that they were not her grandparents. But he'd always been so vital. At seventy, he was as outgoing and full of life as many fifty-year-olds. He was always busy with some activity or other. How could this have happened?

Finally, she pulled herself together, blew her nose, and dialed Brian's number.

Her voice was steady when he answered. "I got a call from Ike."

The what, when, and where questions poured from him. But her somberness soon communicated itself, even over the phone line. It didn't take long to explain. When she'd finished he answered shortly.

"I'll be right there."

And he was. It seemed she'd no sooner replaced the phone on its bedside table than Brian was knocking on her door. No words passed between them.

Brian wrapped Dana in a warm embrace. Her pale face remained dry against his shirt-front, but he held her tightly, right there inside the front doorway, in plain sight of Naomi and whoever else might want to look. His hand ran soothingly over her back as he held her, lending her whatever comfort he could with his steady support.

When he finally felt Dana relax against him, he led her over to the couch. He sat beside her, his arm still solid across her shoulders, while she told him about Ike's call.

"How, Brian? How could this happen without everyone knowing?" *Without me knowing* was what she really wanted to scream. The guilt was almost unbearable. But Brian's presence was making it easier. The tactile comfort she derived from the feel of his arm across her shoulders, his warm hand rubbing her back . . . She'd better watch out.

She looked into Brian's eyes. He was getting harder to see, his face full of shadows as the room darkened. It was late in the evening— that special time of day when the light inside was fading but the outside world was colored by a particular luminescence from the setting sun.

Stalwart Brian tried to answer her unanswerable questions. "It happens sometimes, Dana. We can't always know when or why." *But I wish I did*, Brian added to himself, *so I could help you now*. He tried to reassure her, though the words seemed of little worth. "It wasn't your fault."

This last was pronounced in a voice firm enough to penetrate even Dana's fear-clouded brain. She peered into his face, trying to see through the shadows of dusk, into his eyes, into his brain. Did he mean it?

As Dana leaned toward him, searching his face with an intense look, Brian also moved closer. Her floral scent washed over him with an almost hynotic effect. He lowered his head a fraction more. Her lips were so near. Just a few more inches. They parted, soft and pink and sweet, drawing him irresistibly forward.

And then he touched his lips to hers. The pressure was light, a whisper of a touch. It was everything he'd hoped, and more. His lips moved along the edge of her mouth, then continued upward, feathering light kisses across her cheek. Dana's cheek was soft, her skin cool against the heat of his own.

Brian held her that way for a while, cheek to cheek, inhaling her special fragrance, enjoying the closeness. Finally he trailed his seeking mouth back over to her tantalizing lips.

This time the pressure of his lips against hers was more definite, a light steady pressure that caused delicious sensations for Dana. Her lips opened a little wider, anxious for more. His arms moved around her, drawing her closer. Their embrace was like a joyful harmony.

The kiss deepened. Dana's arms drew him ever nearer. Finally, Brian pulled back. He continued to hold Dana close, his cheek laid against her hair, while he drew great breaths into his lungs.

Steady, he told himself. *Steady*. He couldn't take advantage during such an intensely emotional episode. His brain knew it, but he wished the rest of him knew it.

Dana too was becoming aware of the circumstances and where they could lead. With a sudden motion she pulled away from Brian and wrapped her arms around herself.

They sat together yet apart for a full five minutes, staring into the dark. Thinking. Not thinking. Breathing. Feeling.

Finally, Dana reached over and flipped on the table lamp. "So." Her voice came out thick and sultry, surprising her into starting over. She cleared her throat first. "So," she began again, her voice sounding normal this time. "Do you want to hear the tape from the answering machine?" She slowly turned back to Brian as she spoke. "When you pick up the phone after it starts recording, it usually continues to record."

Dana proved to be right. But listening to the message several times did nothing to help them determine from where the call had originated.

"This is getting us nowhere," Brian finally said. Dana was pale and looked ready to drop.

"It's late and you haven't eaten. Let me get you some soup or something."

He led the way into the kitchen, stopping in the living room en route to ask about the clutter of shopping bags strewn beside the door.

"Oh my gosh, I completely forgot." Dana reached for the bags, pulling them up, replacing items that had fallen out. "I was moving things from my apartment. I heard the phone as I unlocked the door and literally dropped everything so I could go answer it."

Brian stooped to help, his eyes searching out hers. "You're moving back?"

Dana still felt defensive about her choice. It was her own choice, of course, and she was only feeling defensive to herself. "I thought I should. I need to be here when he gets back. And it's almost the end of the month and my landlord has a waiting list for the apartments. So under the circumstances he said I could leave on short notice without penalties. His uncle has Alzheimer's—"

Her babbling had taken them and their parcels as far as her bedroom. Now she dropped everything inside the doorway and blinked frantically against the imminent tears.

Brian dropped his own burden and wrapped her in his arms. He wished she would sob into his shirtfront like she had three days ago. He believed crying helped to get things out; it couldn't be healthy to keep it all locked up inside. But while she hugged him to her, her eyes remained dry. Finally, he held her away from him.

"Now you listen to me, Dana Kapualani Long. Your father's been in good health all this time. From everything I've read, Alzheimer's develops gradually. It doesn't hit all at once like this, with someone fine one day and wandering off lost the next."

Dana nodded, but it was obvious she didn't really believe him. No wonder she was so upset and full of guilt. Why hadn't he realized earlier where that creative mind was leading her?

"Look, it's been a hard day. Let me heat up some soup; and then why don't you do some sketching, or work on Pualani's dress or something for the rest of the night? It will get your mind off all this. Help you relax. Then try to get some sleep."

Dana was still nodding.

"I'll borrow my friend Kimo's truck and help you get the rest of the stuff from your apartment tomorrow. Okay?"

While Brian prepared the soup, Dana went back to her room to unpack some of her things. She knew she was tired because she'd allowed Brian to tell her what to do without a hint of protest. However, she did feel better after their small meal of soup and crackers. While she cleaned up the kitchen, Brian unloaded her drawing table from her car, then helped set it up in the spare room off the kitchen. It was where she already had her sewing machine set up.

Tears once more flooded her vision as she remembered Ike saying he'd leave that room clear—just in case she wanted to move back home. Her mother had used it as her sewing room and he wanted her to make use of it that way too.

Later, as she walked him to the door, Dana's voice turned soft. "I always felt you didn't approve of my career."

Brian looked down at her, brows raised, eyes wide with surprise. "You did?" He shook his head. "It's not that. I always knew you had talent. But I wanted an easier route to success for you—and you chose a difficult one."

He still doesn't get it, Dana thought. "But it was *my* choice."

Silence. Disappointed, she turned her head away and changed the subject.

"Thank you for coming over, Brian. And for making dinner. I appreciate it." A crooked smile turned up the right side of her lips. "I can't seem to remember to eat anymore. I'm lucky to have you around to remind me."

Brian reached up and brushed a stray curl away from her cheek. "Anytime." He was drawn to her, his head moving infinitely closer.

As Brian drew nearer, Dana found herself leaning into him, drawn by the heat of his large frame. She knew he would be warm and solid.

Encouraged, Brian lowered his lips until they touched hers. Feather-light, the kiss was tantalizing, unbearably sweet. As one, they reached for each other, sharing another, deeper kiss.

With a lot of determination and a grim smile, Brian drew back. "Think Naomi is enjoying this?"

Dana grimaced. "Without doubt."

"Better get back inside." He planted another light kiss on her lips. "Go work on your sewing and designing until you're tired enough to sleep."

Dana watched him descend the steps to the driveway and his car.

Until she was tired enough to sleep. Easy for him to say. She doubted she'd ever be tired enough after today's events.

With a final wave as the car backed out of the driveway, Dana closed the door. What had happened to all her anger toward Brian? Instead of meekly heading into the spare room, she should be raging over his telling her what to do. Again.

Was it his charismatic presence or had Brian changed enough to dissipate the anger she'd felt these past two years? He had brought an important client her way. He'd finished painting her walls. And he'd made her dinner. Not takeout; he'd actually gone into the kitchen and heated something up, small though it was.

Dana shrugged as she sat at her drawing board, trying to work the kinks out of tense muscles. Work—she needed to work. *Clear your mind and get to work, Dana Long,* she told herself. That was the only way she'd ever get away from Ike's plaintive voice asking for her mother.

It was already the next morning when Dana finally felt exhausted enough to fall into bed and sleep. She'd spent hours working on Pualani's dress, as well as sketching out other new ideas. The creative frenzy that engulfed her when she began to design and then execute that design was the only thing that could draw her away from her worries.

Exhaustion coupled with the sound of raindrops on the roof finally helped send her into a troubled sleep. As she closed her eyes, her tiredness produced a colored haze against her lids, reminding her of the fabulous rainbow she and Brian had seen four days ago. But the hope she'd felt at its sight seemed to be gone, disintegrated beneath the dismal rains of Hilo.

Dana stood at the kitchen window. She smiled excitedly and waved. There was Ike. He was in the garden. After a week, after all this worry, there he was getting up from weeding the tomatoes. He saw her in the window and waved, a wide smile on his face.

But something was wrong. He started toward the house, but every time he took a step, he had to stop to pull a new weed from his path. He was trying to come toward her. But the weeds kept growing and he kept stopping. He'd never get out of the garden. He'd never reach her in the house.

Suddenly Dana was frightened. She started for the yard herself. She'd go to him. But she couldn't find the door.

Now she was frantic. Where was the door?

A bell rang. Was it a doorbell? Had he found his way to the house? Was there a doorbell when there wasn't a door?

Dana looked out the window again. No, Ike was still in the garden. There were more weeds than ever. But he had a phone! He was calling her on the cordless phone! He'd tell her where the door was!

Searching frantically for the phone, Dana rolled out of bed, landing in a heap of sweat-dampened sheets on the floor beside her bed.

It was a dream—she'd been dreaming! In her relief, it took her another minute to realize that she was still hearing the ringing phone from her dream.

It might be Ike, like in her dream.

She ran into the other room to answer it.

Chapter Seven

Bright sunlight streamed into Ike's bedroom as Dana flew to the pealing phone.

"You find my brudda yet?"

Dana released a long-held breath in a whoosh. So it wasn't Ike after all, just her dear Aunty Ruth. She threw herself down onto the neatly made bed. She probably should have called her yesterday, but why upset her?

"No. He's still gone, Aunty." She released a long sigh. Frustration penetrated across the line.

"No worry, Dana. I had one dream last night. Pretty soon, we goin' to find him. You wait."

"You had a dream too? So did I." But her excitement at the coincidence soon faded. "But mine was really strange. It didn't exactly leave good feelings."

"You listen to your Aunty, Dana. It's goin' to be okay." Without another word, Ruth hung up.

Dana cradled the receiver. She wished she had that cordless phone Ike had used in her dream. Then she could stop these mad scrambles every time the instrument rang. And for the past week, it had been ringing dozens of times a day.

Even as she finished the thought, the newly irritating jangle sounded again. She grabbed for it, picking it up halfway through the first ring.

"How are you?"

Brian's voice was liquid, rolling across the miles, rippling over her, spreading a cool comfort that rapidly warmed.

"Brian." The name was soft on her tongue. "I just woke up." A quick glance toward the clock confirmed it was very late. "Have you heard anything?"

"Nothing yet. But I have a feeling something will happen soon." He must have covered the phone for a minute, because Dana heard some muffled voices at the other end. Then his voice was clear again but businesslike, as though someone was beside him listening in. "Has he called again?"

"No. Just Aunty Ruth. It's funny, but she has

a feeling too. That it will be over soon. I hope you're both right."

"Count on it. Gotta go."

Dana heard the click as he hung up. Honestly, she wasn't getting a chance to say goodbye to anyone today.

Despite her late start and the worry of Ike's continued absence, Dana found herself working at a high level of competence. Pualani stopped in to check on the progress of her dress, declaring herself delighted with the way it was making up. Dana shared the latest news on Ike and displayed some of the new designs she'd created during her long night.

By the time Brian knocked on her door that evening, she was up to her elbows in emerald-colored silk, trying to finish the dress so Pualani could have a final fitting.

"Mom and Vovo sent over some dinner," Brian said, raising his hands to show her a heavy casserole dish. The glass cover rocked at the movement and tantalizing aromas poured forth.

"Mmm." Dana sniffed deeply. "It smells heavenly. Come on in. I've been working on Pualani's dress all day, and I don't remember if I had any lunch."

Brian laughed, but deep inside he mourned

for her. She was aching for her lost father, and doing her best to cope. And he, who should have been able to help her, hadn't been able to do a darn thing. One old man and one small island. The more they searched, the less likely it seemed he had gone off island. Yet no one seemed to know where he could be. And the longer he remained missing, the more Brian suspected there would not be a happy ending.

He wrenched his mind back to the Longs' kitchen. He had to abandon his gloomy thoughts before Dana grew suspicious. "Why don't you get us something to drink? I'll set the table."

After their dinner, Brian suggested a walk. The humid warmth of the tropical afternoon had given way to a clear, cool night. Too numerous to count, the stars twinkled overhead, still bright despite the brilliant three-quarter moon halfway up in the night sky.

Together they walked the block over to the municipal golf course where numerous people throughout the neighborhood made use of the fairways and cart paths for their evening and early-morning strolls. The palm trees rustled softly in the gentle breeze and the call of a cardinal seemed loud in counterpoint.

Dana was intensely aware of the powerful male figure walking sedately beside her. Moon shadows traveled before them, and Dana couldn't help but notice how large and strong his looked beside her petite one.

The path they followed turned and the shadows moved to the side and became one. Dana took a deep breath and reached for Brian's hand. She thought he was probably being very gallant by staying away from her. But right now, she wanted to feel his hard, callused palm against hers, feel the warmth in that hand seep up her arm. The sweater she'd donned before they left might warm her body, but Brian's touch could warm her heart.

Brian felt her hand reach out for his, a silent exultation singing through his soul. Dana was actually reaching out for him again, not just falling against him because of emotional circumstances.

There was something deeply satisfying about walking along holding hands. It was such an old-fashioned thing to do, yet it brought a closeness that couldn't be equaled. Soon they were swinging their arms between them, laughing like children.

Brian stopped, pulling Dana around by her hand until she swung against him. He put his arm around her, pulling her close, keeping their still-entwined hands between them.

The moonlight shone down on her upturned

face, shimmering her hair and sparkling her eyes. Her golden skin glowed with a silvery sheen; her lips were moist and red, full and inviting. He couldn't resist.

The kiss was long and slow and sweet. Dana saw it coming and welcomed it. The tropical night was so sensuous, with its sweet sultry air. The breezes through the palms created a special music, punctuated by the occasional noise of a barking dog or a car on the nearby road. And she could smell Brian's special scent—something spicy and piney and full of memories.

When they finally pulled apart, both were breathless and warm. Slow smiles spread over both mouths.

"That was nice." Dana's voice was so husky she barely recognized it. *Thank goodness for the dark,* she thought as she felt a blush stain her cheeks.

"It was." Brian's voice too was throaty. He wanted to kiss her again, but behind them came the sound of voices as a family walked their dog. Brian released Dana, still keeping hold of her hand, and they turned back the way they'd come.

He left her at the bottom of the stairs without following her back into the house. It might be too difficult to leave if he went inside with her and picked up where they'd been interrupted.

Dana practically floated up the steps and into the house. It was a beautiful night and she felt warm and loved. With her mind temporarily free of her current worries, she drifted into her bedroom and climbed between the sheets.

Dana was in Brian's arms, gliding across an enormous dance floor. Her pink satin dress rustled softly as she moved. Brian was such a wonderful dancer. Held so gently in his strong arms, Dana felt she could dance forever.

Then the music began to change. The quiet strains of old dance favorites turned into noisy rock and roll. They were still moving; she was still in his arms. But the music changed again, to heavy metal. And it got louder, and faster, and louder—

Dana sat up in bed.

Another dream. Yet she was still hearing music.

As she became more alert and the heavy metal faded out of hearing, she realized she'd been awakened by a car stereo. Some teenager, probably, coming home from a date and blaring his radio loud enough to be heard for a mile.

Dana settled back into the pillows. She was dreaming a lot lately. Yesterday's dream was strange enough to leave her slightly shaken, but tonight's just brought memories. A brief smile touched her lips as the sweet strains of the melody from *Cats* drifted through her mind.

Memories. That pink satin dress she'd worn in her dream. It was the one she'd designed for her graduation dance. How she'd looked forward to that night. And it had been everything she'd hoped. She and Brian had danced together all night, lost in a sensual haze as they swayed in each other's arms.

The ring of the telephone jarred Dana out of the past. She glanced over at the clock as she pushed back the covers. Three-thirty A.M. Her heart in her throat, she dashed down the dark hall to Ike's bedroom, catching up the receiver just as the third ring began. At this time of the morning, the news had to be about Ike. And good news rarely came in the dark hours of the early morning.

"Dana!"

In the predawn quiet, Brian's voice came through the receiver loud and clear. Somewhere outside a rooster crowed, the sound in the darkness causing an almost hysterical bubble of laughter which Dana quickly tamped down.

"You found him!" Her voice sounded thick and relief left it soft and breathless. Weak-kneed, she sank down onto the bedroom floor, her body resting against the side of the bed.

But her relief was short-lived.

"We've found his car."

Dana's stomach clenched painfully, almost stopping her breath. At this hour?

"Oh, Brian. Is he . . . ?" Her voice trailed off, afraid to ask the all-important question.

"Just his car, Dana. He wasn't in it. It was way out in Waimea—on a narrow road in the middle of nowhere. It was out of gas. They found it at this hour because some *paniolo* was coming home late from a party and crashed into it. He'd been drinking—but he was responsible enough to report it when he got back to the ranch. He hadn't seen anyone, but just in case, he didn't want to leave someone stranded."

Tears were streaming down her cheeks, but Dana wiped them away furiously. "So what now?"

"The Waimea police will start looking for him as soon as it's light. They're already organizing the search party. I'll pick you up in half an hour and we'll head out there. Dress warmly." He paused. "Okay?"

Dana blinked back another bout of tears and let out a breath she hadn't realized she'd been holding. At least she wouldn't have to fight with him about going along to help in the search.

She didn't even mind that he was ordering her around again. He was trying; that was what that last question was all about. "Okay."

Dana was ready and waiting when Brian arrived. As they had done once before, they drove through Hilo toward the Hamakua coast road. So early in the day, the Hilo streets were dark and eerily deserted. Things seemed unfamiliar in the artificial light, so different from the intense tropical sun. Reflections from the streetlights sparkled in the raindrops and shimmered in puddles, lending a bizarre sort of party air to the desolate city.

Brian urged Dana to nap, but she was too excited at the prospect of finding Ike after their long search and too tense at the thought of him wandering about in the cold, wet foothills.

It had been a week, actually eight whole days, that he'd been gone. No one had seen him since he left Martin Chung's house early last Thursday morning. Where was he all that time? Where was he now?

As they headed north along the coastal highway, the sun began to rise—coming up out of the ocean in a glorious burst of brilliance. Dana sighed with pleasure at the beautiful display. Even Brian took his attention from the road long enough to appreciate nature's gift.

In quiet peace they continued their journey.

* * *

The blue Taurus looked small and forlorn, pulled to the far right of a narrow dirt road that ran through rich green pastureland. Its once bright paint was dull with dust and the rear fender was crumbled, broken bits of red glass from the taillight littering the ground.

Dana stood beside Brian, her eyes dry, her back straight. He thought she must be churning inside, but she looked calm and controlled. Her reddened eyes with their dark shadows were the only indication of turmoil.

He reached out, hesitated, then placed his hands firmly around hers. Her hands felt small and very cold and he held them for a moment, hoping to lend her some warmth.

"The local police have already started a search for him," Brian told her. "They have *paniolos* from all the surrounding ranches out."

He watched Dana's face for some reaction, but she continued to stare out at the surrounding landscape. Brian was concerned. Was she all right? What else could he do?

Dana could see some of the volunteer cowboys roaming the hills. The cool drizzle, little more than a mist, felt good on her face, but it could mean problems for someone Ike's age. Would he have a jacket or a sweater?

With an effort, she pushed her worry aside.

If these men could use their valuable time to search for her father, she had to be alert enough to thank them. Looking at the hilly terrain it was obvious that the searchers on horseback were the ideal people to conduct the search. He was probably on foot and he could be anywhere.

She forced a smile as she turned to Brian. "Thank you," she whispered. She turned her hands, still trapped between his, until she could give him a squeeze. Brian squeezed back.

Brian wanted to remain at her side, hold her tight, and guard her from more serious worries. But he moved off to confer with the officer in charge, hoping to get some information for Dana.

As Brian moved away, Dana's attention was drawn to a *paniolo* leading three horses and coming right toward her.

"Rusty!" Dana threw her arms around her cousin. "Is one of those for me?" The haunted look left her eyes, replaced by determination.

Rusty nodded. "I figured you'd want to search too."

Dana was so touched she could hardly speak. She stood on tiptoes to plant a kiss on Rusty's cheek. "You figured right. I was afraid I'd have to hang around here all day and I wasn't looking forward to it. Thank you."

By the time he'd helped her mount, Brian was beside them, taking over the third horse.

"Brian. I didn't know you could ride."

Brian looked slightly sheepish. "Well, I don't much, but I can manage. And I wanted to help."

Dana's face lit up with the realization of what he'd done. "You called Rusty, didn't you? To have him meet us with the horses."

Brian remained silent, hoping he had done the right thing, but Rusty answered for him.

"He did. Woke me at three-forty A.M. But I'm glad to do it, Dana."

Dana's eyes locked on Brian's, conveying her love in that single look. But her voice spoke to both men. "Thank you." The words were simple but they said it all.

As they moved away from the area around the abandoned Taurus, Dana felt the pleasure of being on horseback after such a long time. She'd be sore tomorrow, but the terrain here was beautiful, the drizzle too light to be bothersome, and the sun was attempting to break through, casting rainbows over the land. Soon someone would spot Ike wandering in a pasture, and it would all be over.

But despite the possible good omens of the rainbows, they did not find Ike that day. The searchers returned at dusk, tired and hungry, prepared to go home and rest and return again the next day to resume the search.

Dana and Brian accepted Rusty's hospitality and spent the evening with him. Pam had a large, hearty meal ready when they returned, after which she and Rusty left their guests to themselves.

Exhausted from a long day of riding, long-unused muscles aching, Dana soaked in a hot tub until the water turned cold. She hadn't done any riding for years, and while she could still handle a horse, her muscles were loudly pro-fjtesting the hours in the saddle. She suspected Brian was feeling the same way. He ran a bath for himself the moment she vacated the tub.

Everyone went to bed early. Dana felt lucky to be so exhausted. There was no other way she'd ever be able to sleep otherwise. If she allowed herself to think she would surely shrivel up and die from the uncertainty and the pain. The night had turned cool after an early-evening shower, and Ike was out there somewhere—cold, alone, and probably wet.

Tears dampened her pillow before exhaustion sent Dana into a restless slumber.

Dana stood at the kitchen window again. She smiled and waved. There was Ike, in the garden.

But wait. It wasn't the garden. The backyard had changed into a pasture. Dana saw Ike walking through it. He seemed to be looking for someone.

Dana waved frantically, but he didn't see her. He kept walking, looking.

Dana shouted, "Here I am, Daddy! I'm here." But he didn't seem to hear her. He just continued to move. Looking, looking.

Suddenly Dana saw a large bull in the pasture. Ike was moving right toward it.

"Daddy! Daddy! Watch out!"

But he didn't hear her. He didn't see the bull. He kept walking toward it.

"Daddy!"

Dana sat up in bed, her borrowed nightshirt damp with sweat. The dream . . . It was just a dream.

Dana took deep breaths of the cold night air, calming her racing heart. Gray fingers of early light were already penetrating the jalousies, so she threw back the covers. No need to try to get more rest; the search would resume at sunrise.

It was going to be another long, difficult day. As usual for the area, it began with a cool drizzle. Rusty, Brian, and Dana continued the search together. By mid-morning the sun was peeking out of the white clouds; blue sky appeared, and a huge rainbow.

Dana steeled herself against the beauty. She wanted to believe in the rainbow, but she'd been let down twice already.

Dana reined in her horse, taking a moment to have a sip of water and look around. Rusty and Brian pulled up on either side of her.

"Looks pretty good, eh?" Rusty said. "I never get tired of looking at this land. And all the time we have rainbows."

Brian murmured an agreement but Dana just nodded, following the arc of the rainbow to its end in the next pasture. Its beauty was irresistible.

Rusty was still talking. "Look at that rainbow. It seems so close, like I could just reach out and touch it. Or find that pot of gold . . ."

Dana stood in her stirrups, staring at the fading end of the rainbow. What was that?

She strained her eyes toward the next pasture where the rainbow disappeared in a small stand of eucalyptus. There was something there, she was sure of it. And it wasn't a pot of gold.

Trying not to get too excited, she started forward, stopping again a little closer to get a better look. The rainbow was gone now, moved back to the next pasture to touch a small creek bed. But the anomaly she'd noted was still there.

"Brian, Rusty, look. There at the base of the eucalyptus. Is that an aloha shirt?"

They looked where she pointed. But before either man even got out his agreement, the three of them were galloping across the rolling landscape toward the man in the blue aloha shirt lying beneath the trees. Brian lagged behind as he took out a walkie-talkie to contact the base camp.

By the time the three arrived at the small thicket, the man had risen to his feet and started to walk toward them.

Dana watched him as she approached, a small chill moving up her back. *It's my dream*, she thought. *He's wandering through the pasture, just like my dream.*

Then she was beside him, dismounting, taking him in her arms. This time the tears running down her cheeks were tears of happiness.

Ike returned her fierce hug with a weak one.

"Rose." He rubbed his cheek against her hair and squeezed her tight. "I've been looking for you, Rose."

The relief that so recently filled Dana receded. Dread wrapped its icy tentacles around her body and squeezed her midsection as she heard her father call her by her mother's name. "It's all right. I'm right here."

Ike's voice matched his frail appearance. "I knew I'd find you at Aunty Lily's. You always liked to ride her horses."

Dana kept her arms around her father even as she raised her head. Brian was busy on his walkie-talkie, so she turned to Rusty. "He's so cold."

"Here, wrap this around him." He handed her a blanket he had retrieved from his saddle-bags.

Dana wrapped the rough wool around Ike's shoulders, feeling like a mother tending a small child. How could she not have noticed how Ike had aged? He was so frail. Was it just the experience of the past week, or was this something else she'd missed? The guilt she'd worked so hard to vanquish returned with a vengeance.

Keeping her arms firmly around her father, Dana closed her eyes and silently said a heartfelt prayer of thanks.

Chapter Eight

"Wassa matter you? Got to eat. Got to keep your strength up."

Dana smiled at the bullying from Aunty Ruth. She knew Ruth was worried about her baby brother, and trying not to show it. Dana had managed a nap when they returned to the Longs' from the hospital, but Ruth had spent all her time in the kitchen, cooking away her troubles.

Ruth brought over a bowl of saimin and set it before Dana, then returned to the stove to remove a pan of cinnamon rolls from the oven. They were waiting for Brian. Ike had been brought in to Hilo Medical Center and was being well cared for by a variety of specialists. But Dana and Ruth had only each other—and Brian.

Late last night, the hospital staff had shooed them out and told them not to return until the doctor called; they all, Ike included, needed rest more than anything else. One of the nurses who had gone to high school with Dana told her Ike would probably sleep through most of the next few days. There was no point to them just hanging around while the tests were being done.

"Where's yours, Aunty Ruth?" Dana asked. Ruth placed a heaping plate of cinnamon rolls in the center of the table but sat down without a bowl or plate of her own. "Don't you have to keep your strength up too?"

"Bah!" Ruth patted her ample stomach. "I got plenty strength here in reserve."

Dana played with her spoon, moving it through the clear broth, finally filling it with noodles. "Where do you think he was all that time?" Although Dana had stayed with him for hours after his recovery, Ike had been in no condition to explain anything.

The sound of tires on the graveled drive had both women leaping up. But Ruth gave Dana a firm look. "You eat. I'll get it."

Within moments she was back in the kitchen with Brian. Dana gave up the pretense of eating and pushed the bowl away. "Do you have any news?"

Ruth ladled out another bowl of saimin and

placed it before Brian. "You eat while you talk. Got to keep your strength up."

Dana rolled her eyes at what was becoming Aunty Ruth's favorite expression.

"Did you find out where he's been?" Even as she asked the question, Dana took a closer look at Brian and felt her heart roll over. His eyes were bloodshot and his chin was shadowed by dark stubble. "Oh, Brian," she added, "you'd better eat first." She pushed the plate of warm rolls over in front of him. "Have you been home at all since yesterday?"

Brian dipped his spoon gratefully into the soup, smiling slightly at Dana's concern. He was starved. Using clues found in Ike's car they'd managed to trace back his activities and fill in the missing days. But first . . .

He replaced his spoon after just one sip, though the rich aroma of the rolls was causing rumblings from his empty stomach.

"Before I forget . . ." Brian reached into a paper bag he'd put down on the table when he came in. He removed a worn and faded red cardboard box and handed it to Dana.

Dana sucked in her breath and Ruth sighed.

"Where did you find it?" Dana asked as she uncovered the box and pulled out the thin album. Lovingly turning the pages, she gazed at the little bits of colored paper which had been used to mail letters a hundred years ago in the Hawaiian kingdom. Some of her ancestors might have affixed these same stamps to a treasured letter.

"It was under the front seat in the Taurus, shoved way back so it wasn't apparent with a quick look."

Dana smiled as she returned the album to its box. "That's what he does when he takes it somewhere." A brief excitement brightened her eyes. "And it means he was thinking clearly when he put it there. It's always been his method of theft prevention, to hide things way under the front seat."

Ruth, still standing behind Dana, put her hand on her niece's shoulder. "He goin' be okay, girl."

For a few minutes there was silence in the kitchen as Brian ate and the women thought of a wonderful old man.

When Brian put his spoon down beside an empty bowl, he felt revitalized. Thanking both Ruth and Dana for the meal brought them out of their reverie. Then he removed a small notebook from his pocket and turned toward Dana.

"We found out where Ike has been for the past week."

Dana pulled herself up straighter in the hard

kitchen chair, all her attention focused on Brian. "Where?"

Ruth sat down, drawing her chair up close to the table to listen.

"Well"—he nodded toward Dana—"you found out he spent Wednesday night in Honomu with Martin Chung. We assumed he was heading out to the Mauna Kea Beach Hotel to visit Cal Coolidge when he left there. Apparently he stopped in Honokaa to see Johnny Jardine."

"Oh!"

Brian looked up at Dana's exclamation.

"I tried calling him several times, but he was never home."

"Exactly. It seems Johnny's twelve-year-old grandson is here from the mainland visiting him. He took him out fishing. They were just packing up to leave when Ike arrived on Thursday. His boat sleeps four, so they invited Ike to join them. Johnny lent him some clothes and he went. They left from Kawaihae Thursday afternoon and were gone all week."

Brian shot the two women a sympathetic look. One simple phone call could have eliminated a week of stress and worry. "Johnny felt real bad when he heard what had happened. He had a radio, but they never used it for anything more than weather updates. And we never found Ike's car because he pulled it into their carport before they left."

Dana was still trying to take it all in.

"Fishing!" Off on a boat—she could hardly believe it. She'd never even considered that as a possibility.

"Ike always like to fish," Ruth muttered as she rose from the table. She started to clean up the dishes, but then looked between the two young people. She put the bowls and flatware into the sink and turned toward the back door. "I think I go mow the grass."

And she was gone, mumbling beneath her breath about the length of the grass in the yard.

Brian looked at Dana and lowered his voice to a stage whisper. "I think she's giving us a chance to be alone together."

One corner of Dana's lips tipped upward as though she was trying not to laugh. "Terribly obvious, isn't she?" She reached over and took his hand. His warm strength flowed into her as she held onto him. Then she grinned. "But why disappoint her?"

Brian grinned back before his expression turned serious. He scrutinized Dana's face, trying hard to see beneath the smiling facade. She seemed to be handling everything well. But the uncertainty of Ike's condition would not have eliminated all the tension of the past week. "How are you, Dana? Really?"

"Pretty good. It's such a relief to have Dad back. Even though we don't know yet . . ."

Brian rose, pulling her up with him. He enfolded her in his gentle embrace, resting his cheek against her fragrant hair. They clung together for a long moment, enjoying the feel of being in each other's arms.

I can get used to this again, Dana thought. *In fact, I have gotten used to it, just this past week.* She started to pull away, but stopped with her hands on his chest, his arms still loosely around her. She'd just noticed Brian's face; he looked ready to drop from fatigue.

"You need to go home and get some sleep." She reached up to smooth some hairs back from his forehead. "And a hot bath. I'll bet you're still sore from the horseback riding."

Brian grimaced. "Let's just say I discovered a few new muscles these last couple of days."

"I know what you mean." Dana laughed as she led him through the house to the front door. "Go home. Rest. Soak. Let your mom and Vovo fuss over you a little."

Brian gathered her into his arms again. "Okay. But first—"

He pulled her close and lowered his lips.

Dana felt the scratch of his unshaven cheek

on her smooth one, the warmth of his breath on her skin. But his lips when they found hers were smooth and cool.

The first quick kiss turned into a longer, warmer one. Dana's fingers crept up into his hair, weaving through the thick strands. She pulled away with reluctance.

Brian looked down at Dana's beautiful face. She too had shadows under her eyes, faint purplish smudges that looked like wrongly placed eye makeup. And now her cheeks were reddened from his unshaven beard. He felt a tightness in his chest as he realized how little he could do to help her.

He dropped another kiss on the top of her head and moved toward the door. "You need some rest yourself, Dana. And maybe a soak in a hot tub," he added.

As he walked down the steps to his car he called back, "I'll see you later at the hospital."

While Brian caught up on some much-needed sleep, Dana went into the spare room. She would have to start thinking of it as her sewing room now. As in her mother's day, a large rectangular table filled most of the small room. Her Bernina sat at one end, while a cutting board covered the rest of the table. Spread over the cutting board was the emerald-green silk of Pualani's dress.

Dana stood in the small room pressing her lips together as she felt the frustration of being right back where she'd started. She'd finally moved away from this house where she'd always felt so stifled.

She didn't blame Ike and Rose. They'd tried for years to have a child, but they were well into middle age when she finally came along. It was truly a sign of their love that they'd kept her so close. Was it any wonder that she'd been unable to handle a closer relationship with Brian at that time? He looked after her with the same possessiveness that Ike had. It had all gotten to be too much.

Dana walked over to the table and touched the beautiful green silk. Well, she might be home again, but things were different now. She was no longer a young student, dependent on Ike for her every need. She had been on her own for two years. She had a profession. She smiled at the word. Brian might think she was just a seamstress, but she had always considered her work a profession. She did good work and she was proud of it.

A frown wrinkled her forehead as she sat down before the sewing machine. Of course, Brian had recommended her to Pualani for this important commission. And there were other indications that he'd changed. Maybe their relationship could develop into something more.

Dana smiled as she picked up her needle and thread to finish the handwork on the silk dress. Brian might have changed, but his kisses hadn't. They were as good as ever.

Early that evening, Dana, Ruth, and Brian returned to Hilo Medical Center.

Dana had to blink back her tears when she entered her father's room, though she smiled when she noticed Aunty Ruth doing the same. Ike lay amid the white sheets looking pale, old, and very frail. His eyes seemed to have sunk into his head, and his hair looked thinner than it had a week ago. An intraveneous tube was attached to his arm, immobilized against the side rail of the bed.

Ike remained asleep as his visitors arranged themselves around the bed. Brian stood close beside Dana, his arm resting lightly against her back in case she felt the need of his support.

Brian's presence sustained Dana during the short visit. She held her father's hand while she said some silent prayers. It was impossible to tell how he was doing by watching him sleep. He just looked tired and old.

The tears came, and Dana had to blink rapidly to keep them from spilling down her cheeks.

Several minutes into their silent vigil, a nurse entered the room to check on Ike. "He's doing fine," she assured them. "He's not in a coma, he's just sleeping. He needs lots of rest after his adventure. And the medication is also making him sleep."

The nurse busied herself taking his pulse and blood pressure, then straightened out the bedclothes. Before leaving the room she urged them all to go home.

"We'll call if there's any change at all. It'll be easier for you to wait at home. And you want to be well rested and healthy yourselves when he finally wakes up."

Dana thought it was hard to argue with that.

"Shouldn't you be at the hospital with your father?"

Dana and Malia were working together to dress a life-sized mannequin in a white satin *holoku*. Malia asked her question as the shiny fabric slid down over the hips of the figure and Dana stepped back to admire the effect.

Lokelani's was almost ready to open; only the cosmetic touches were left, like dressing the mannequin for the street window and hanging some pictures on the walls.

"No. I do go over every day. But he's always sleeping. Or off having tests." She and Malia moved the mannequin into place in the large glass window, then Dana lowered herself to the floor to adjust the satin train to its best advantage. "Actually, the nurses and doctors urged me to go on with everyday activities. And being down here getting things ready, or being home sewing . . ." She let her voice trail off as she stood back up. "It all helps me keep my mind off my worries. And I can be there in minutes if he should need me."

Malia set a lei of white silk blossoms around the mannequin's head, fussing with the wig to be sure the hair looked natural. "Those tests they're doing—I guess it takes a while to get the results."

"Yes. And it's not easy waiting."

Satisfied that the bridal *holoku* showed to advantage, Dana pulled a sheer gray curtain across the back of the window, closing off the view of the street. She stepped over to the entrance to survey the room while Malia moved a large fern into place beside the curtain.

"It looks good."

Malia joined Dana in the doorway, giving the room a quick once-over. Comfortable upholstered furniture slipcovered in flowered fabric was arranged in a conversational grouping in the main room of the store. The sheer curtain kept people passing on the street from seeing inside while creating a fine backdrop for the gown displayed in the outside window. Potted plants gave a homey feel, and fashion and bridal magazines were arranged on the coffee table before the sofa. The rest of the store, which comprised the main work area, was out of sight behind a gray fabric screen.

"Yep. This is where people entering will get their first impression. And I like it." Malia turned to Dana and gave her an impulsive hug. "It looks terrific, Dana. It's going to be great."

Dana returned the hug, but wished she could feel as confident as her loyal assistant. "I hope so. Honestly, Malia, the closer I get to opening day, the more nervous I get about the whole thing."

Malia laughed. "Normal, I'd say. But let's leave everything for now and go next door for some coffee." She shooed Dana out the door then led the way to the restaurant next door. "Did you know they have sinfully delicious desserts here?"

Brian smiled to himself as he pulled into the parking lot at Hilo Medical Center. Ike was back, he and Dana were reestablishing their relationship, and the world had become a rosier place. His life hadn't looked this good since the night he'd achieved his bachelor's degree.

What a great year that was—finally getting his degree after years of part-time studies and night school. A wonderful girlfriend. A promising future in the party. He'd looked forward to marriage and a family.

Then Dana had gotten so riled up when he suggested she see his pal at E.L.M. about a job. He'd planned to propose that night, had made arrangements to choose a diamond ring with her the next day.

She'd been talking about the new job she'd be starting in a week—telling him she was a little nervous. So he'd told her about this opportunity—to get a better paying job. Something with more possibilities for the future.

And she'd exploded! At first he thought it was just nerves—graduation night, going out to face the world. It was a tense time.

But when she threw the pikake lei at him . . .

He got angry then, and for months dated anyone and everyone. And hoped Dana would call. But of course his rapid dating of other women didn't help the situation.

He still wasn't sure he understood what happened that night. But he knew he still loved Dana.

As the elevator took him up to her, he reflected on the current situation. Ike hadn't been very lucid when they found him, and the hospital staff said he continued to have episodes of vagueness. Brian had consulted his friend Frank Low. *Dr.* Frank Low, who worked almost exclusively with older people at a care home outside Hilo. Of course, Frank had told him he couldn't diagnose from his description, but he'd offered possibilities. And most of them weren't good. But he had said that he would make room for Ike at the care home—right away if necessary. Or as soon as he was released from the hospital.

Brian smiled again as he rode the elevator upward. It was the perfect solution to Dana's problems. If Ike was as sick as he appeared, Dana wouldn't be able to take care of him on her own. She'd be glad to hear there was an option. And a good one. Frank's care home was one of the best in the state.

The elevator doors slid open and Brian saw Dana. She stood at the end of the hall, speaking to one of the nurses.

He greeted her with a hug. Her eyes were huge in her pale face, dark shadows still purplish beneath her eyes. But even now a bright hope burned deep within her; he could see it reflected in the depths of her eyes. And she returned his hug—with enthusiasm, he thought.

"How is he?"

Dana smiled. " 'Resting comfortably.' " It was obviously a direct quote. "Anyway, he's asleep and I thought I'd get some coffee."

Brian raised his hand to show her a small paper bag she hadn't noticed he was carrying. "I brought you a banana smoothie."

Dana's face was transformed as the tiredness was erased by a wide smile. "You angel!" she cried, reaching for the moisture-laden paper cup he handed her.

Even tired, Brian thought, Dana was beautiful. Especially when she smiled at him that way. He reached into the bag for the paper-wrapped straw.

Dana pushed open the door to Ike's room, lowering her voice. "We can wait in here. He's got to wake up sometime."

She led Brian to two plastic chairs set away from the bed at the end of the room. "I'm really worried about him, Brian. What if he never gets any better?"

Brian almost couldn't hide his smile. Finally, he'd be able to help Dana. Here was the perfect opportunity for him to tell her about Frank Low and his care home. Following her lead, he lowered his voice. "I have some good news."

Dana popped the straw through the plastic top and took a long sip of the thick drink. "I could use some. The doctors are hopeful but they aren't saying much. They're waiting for test results from Honolulu. They keep telling me they're optimistic but it's pretty hard for me to be right now."

So Brian proceeded to tell her about his friend Frank and the wonderful care home he ran. And how he would be willing to take Ike in at any time.

Dana's reaction wasn't what he'd expected. There were no quiet thank-yous, no smiles of relief. She just stared at him, momentarily speechless.

Dana swallowed, the sweet taste of the smoothie that lingered in her mouth suddenly making her feel nauseated. She'd thought Brian had changed. She'd thought they were getting on so well together. Heaven help her, she'd even been thinking of a future for them, together.

But for him to suggest such a thing—putting Ike in a home!

Anger replaced the shock, and she lit into him.

"A home! He's not going to a home!" Her voice was starting to rise, and she cast a quick glance at the bed. Ike continued to sleep, undisturbed by the frantic conversation taking place nearby.

She lowered her voice.

"He's my father."

Brian, amazed by Dana's strong reaction, hardly knew what to say. "But, Dana, if his condition doesn't improve, you won't be able to—"

"I'll do whatever I have to. The doctors say it's too soon to know, but they're optimistic."

Brian heard the resolve in her voice, saw the determination in her eyes.

"It's your decision, Dana." He'd meant to continue on with his own hopes for Ike's recovery but Dana cut him short.

"You're right. It *is* my decision—only mine. And maybe Aunty Ruth's," she added. "I don't recall asking for your help."

She took another quick look over at Ike, who'd moved restlessly, then turned back to Brian.

"I'm an adult but you still treat me like a child. Just because you're a few years older . . ."

"Now wait a minute . . ."

"No. You're doing it to me again, just like you did two years ago. You want to tell me how to do everything. You don't give me credit for being able to make my own decisions. You're worse than my parents."

Dana heard her last sentence and gasped, her hand flying up to cover her mouth.

Brian stared at her, his mouth set in a grim

line. "So that's what this is all about. That's what it's always been about, isn't it? You think Ike was too strict. That's why you wanted to move out." He looked away from her to the frail old man lying on the bed. His eyes came back to rest on Dana's face. He wanted to take her hand but he knew she'd never allow it. But his voice softened. "I'm not your parent, Dana. All I ever wanted to do was keep you safe and make you happy."

Dana closed her eyes and took a deep breath. Her heart was beating wildly from the strong emotion this long-delayed argument was generating. "I know, Brian. But the point is, I don't need you to keep me safe. Especially if it means I can't do anything I want to because it might be dangerous in your eyes. I had enough of that growing up."

She took another deep breath. *Calm down, girl*, she told herself, *calm down*. She had to keep her voice low and quiet. She didn't want to disturb Ike. "I understand how it was with Mom and Dad. They waited so long to have a baby, and they knew there wouldn't be another one. Mom was never quite well again afterward. Do you know the guilt that caused me as a child—thinking that I was responsible for my mother's constant illnesses?"

Brian thought his heart might break at the

forlorn tone he heard in Dana's voice. How could he have known her all this time and not realized how much guilt she carried around with her about her childhood?

Dana thought she was getting off the point, but now that she'd started, she wanted to say it all. She took a long, steadying breath before continuing. "Anyway, it was hard not being able to do the things my friends were doing, because Mom and Dad worried so much about me." Dana's voice grew even softer, so that Brian had to strain to hear her. "I was twelve before I finally learned how to swim, and I never did learn how to roller skate. I didn't get a bicycle till I was in high school. I only learned how to ride one because I used to sneak practice rides on my friends'."

Brian sat quietly beside her. She could tell he didn't know what to do to console her. Finally, he put his hand on her shoulder, a comforting weight that had her wanting to leap up into his arms. But that would never do. Instead, she put his hand away from her and rose to her feet.

"Thank you for the smoothie, Brian." Her voice was dull, her expression blank. She stepped toward the door, pulling it open a crack. "I think you'd better go."

Brian hated to oblige, leaving things between

them like this. But Dana was so upset he decided it would be best to do as she requested. She needed some time alone. Things might get even worse if he stayed any longer.

Dana watched the door close behind him before moving her chair closer to Ike's bed. Her eyes rested on her father but she didn't really see him. In her mind, she was replaying the scene with Brian. Her anger dissipated, replaced by hurt and disappointment. She might not need him to keep her safe. But to make her happy? Would she ever be happy again?

Still, how could he suggest putting her father in a home? It would kill Ike being cooped up in a small room every day. He needed his house, his garden, his hobbies. Brian of all people should understand too, since he lived with his mother and his grandmother. She'd never heard him suggest *they* enter a home.

Dana reached over and took Ike's hand in hers. It felt smaller than she remembered, frailer.

"Don't worry, Dad. I won't let you down. I'll take care of you."

She held on to his hand, running her fingers lightly over the papery skin. She was blinking back her threatening tears, and almost missed it. Almost.

Ike blinked too.

Fastening her eyes on his, holding her breath in anticipation of his finally awakening in her presence, Dana watched as he blinked again. And opened his eyes.

Ike's eyes traveled slowly across the room before settling on her face. She sent up a silent prayer as she offered him a loving smile.

A faint smile tugged at Ike's lips. His voice was hoarse and cracked and very low. But Dana heard him quite distinctly.

"Dana."

Now the tears did come, and Dana had to blink rapidly to keep them from spilling down her cheeks. He knew her. He really knew her!

"Dad." Relief and love poured out in her voice. She gave him a wide smile. "I hear you went fishing."

Ike nodded. "Hadn't been . . . for a long time."

Dana squeezed his hand. "I hope you had a good time."

"Yes." Ike closed his eyes. "So tired."

"I can't stay. You need to rest." Dana patted his shoulder, then leaned over to kiss his dry cheek. By the time she stepped away from the bed, his eyes were closed and he appeared to have dropped back to sleep.

Dana hurried from the room, wiping at her damp cheeks, anxious to report to one of the doctors.

Chapter Nine

Dana pulled up the zipper of the green silk dress and stood aside while Pualani admired it in the mirror. They were in the master bedroom of the Yoshiyamas' home where Dana had come with the almost-completed dress for a final fitting.

"Oh, Dana." Pualani turned from side to side, admiring the way the lovely green silk draped across her body. "This is the loveliest formal dress I've ever had. I'll be the envy of every other woman at that fund-raiser."

Dana was still examining the dress with a critical eye. "I think it's okay, except for right here." She pinched about a half inch of fabric just above Pualani's hip, then looked at her reflection in the mirror and smiled. "Much better."

Pualani laughed. "I thought it looked great before."

"I'll fix that and mark the hem now and I'll have it done for you by tomorrow."

As Dana knelt beside her with a ruler and pincushion, Pualani continued to admire the shimmering emerald fabric. "I can't tell you how glad I am that Brian told me about you. Is your shop open yet?"

Dana smiled. "This coming weekend. I'm having a grand-opening celebration on Friday evening. Why don't you and Sam come?"

"Thanks. We will." Pualani smiled down at Dana, a warm knowing smile. "I guess Brian will be there."

Dana's answer surprised her.

"I wouldn't know."

She kept her head bowed over the hem so Pualani couldn't see her face and the tears that threatened whenever she thought of Brian. That just the memory of him should upset her so easily angered her almost as much as the remembrance of their last conversation.

Dana stuck the next pin in so viciously, she stabbed her finger and had to put it in her mouth to stop the blood before it spilled onto the silk fabric.

"Uh-oh. Lovers' quarrel?"

Dana sat back on her heels and looked up at

Pualani. "No. Definitely not a lovers' quarrel. Just a plain old-fashioned argument."

"Want to talk about it?"

Dana examined her finger to check that the bleeding had stopped, then bent back to her task. "Not really."

But as she moved around to pin the back, she couldn't help commenting, "Brian is just such an old woman sometimes. He wants to protect me—from what, I don't know. He doesn't want me to do anything or go anywhere."

Pualani's eyebrows raised up as her eyes widened with surprise. "Goodness. I know he has some old-fashioned ideas . . ."

Dana let out a short harsh laugh. "I'll say. He thinks because he's a man and I'm a woman he has to make all the difficult decisions for me. It's why we broke up before, you know. He was trying to direct my career. *My* career." Then she added in a calmer voice, "My life."

Pualani looked thoughtful as Dana finished pinning the hem, then helped her step carefully out of the dress so as not to disturb any of the pins. Dana packed it carefully in tissue while Pualani donned a short muumuu.

"I can't believe Brian would be like that," Pualani finally murmured. "He might be old-fashioned, but he's not archaic."

Dana put the large box under her arm and

started for the door. "Well, he's gotten better, but he actually came over to the hospital yesterday and told me he could get Dad into a wonderful nursing home. A nursing home!"

Dana's voice was horrified, just as it had been last night when Brian first suggested it.

Pualani put her arm around Dana and walked with her to the front door. "Don't be too hard on him. I'm sure he thought he was doing you a favor, lining it up in case you needed it. You know, Brian has been taking care of his mother and grandmother for a long time. He was still a boy, really, when his father died, and he gave up his dream of college and law school to become a policeman and help support them. Protecting the women he cares about just comes naturally to him."

Dana stared at Pualani. The other woman was far enough away, emotionally, to look at the situation objectively. Her angle was certainly something to think about. And Dana realized she would never be able to view Brian impartially.

She used her free arm to give Pualani a hug. "I'll think over what you said. I'll see you tomorrow. And don't forget about Friday."

Brian entered Lokelani's with a woman on each arm. Geraldine and Bernice wore their

best Sunday muumuus and had insisted that
he wear one of his nicest shirts. He might not
be sure of his own welcome tonight, but he was
certain Dana would treat his family well. In
fact he was grateful to her. He couldn't remember when Mom and Vovo had been so excited
about something.

Lokelani's looked wonderful. The pale pink
walls he'd helped paint glowed in the soft lighting like the inside of a perfect shell. The front
of the store looked like someone's living room,
with its conversational grouping of overstuffed
furniture.

A gray fabric screen separated the comfortable business area from the more practical
work space. The larger work area was where
Dana and Malia had set up the party—on the
tables which would later be covered with fabrics, patterns, and sewing machines.

After an admiring look around the room,
Brian's mother and grandmother pulled him
over to a glass display case and pointed excitedly to several items.

"That's the ring bearer's pillow I crocheted,"
Bernice informed him.

Brian dutifully examined the item indicated.
Not his style, of course, but pretty nonetheless.

"And there's the heart-shaped pillow I em-
broidered." Geraldine pointed. "The one with

the heart-shaped flower wreath. Dana says these are mainly samples right now, to see what people will want," she told him. "I've already started embroidering another one."

Bernice pointed to what Brian thought looked like tiny little pillows decorated with flowers in a variety of styles and colors. "And we made these little sachets too," she said.

"Ah, right. Very nice, Mom, Vovo," Brian said. What on earth were sachets? he wondered. If Dana was still talking to him maybe he could ask her.

He no sooner thought of Dana than she appeared before them, a wide smile on her face and a bright sparkle in her eye. He hadn't seen her since the disaster of Tuesday evening, and he noticed how much better she looked. The dark shadows beneath her eyes were finally gone and it was good to see the ready smile on her lips.

"Bernice, Geraldine. I'm so glad you could come." She turned toward Brian, but didn't greet him with the enthusiasm she'd shown his mother and grandmother. However, she was determined not to let their disagreement spoil this special day for her. So she greeted him with a smile. "Hello, Brian."

She turned toward the display case, one arm hooked around the waist of each of the older ladies. "Your things look so good! I've had a lot of people ask who made them."

Bernice and Geraldine stood beside her but exchanged a speaking look behind her back. Brian saw them communicating with raised brows, frowns, and head shakes. He hadn't said anything about the quarrel he and Dana had had and he'd been busy, working overtime most days. But it was obvious they'd picked up on some of the tension between them and wanted to know what was going on.

But Dana was talking merrily about the items in the display case, not letting them say much about anything else. Finally, she moved on to another topic.

"I have the most wonderful news too. I spoke to the doctors this afternoon." Her eyes sought Brian's above the women's heads. She might be angry with him, but he deserved to hear her news. "The results of the tests are back. It's not Alzheimer's."

Geraldine and Bernice made the appropriate noises, but Brian just looked into her eyes and smiled. Dana's arms dropped and she found herself clasping her hands in front of her, trying to keep herself from shaking from the force of the emotions rocking through her.

With just that one look, Brian had touched

her right down to her toes. She could feel his relief, his joy for her at this verdict.

She glanced down for a moment to recollect herself, then looked back up, her smile once again in place. "I don't remember all their fancy words, but their tests showed that he had two serious medical problems that caused the delirium—high blood pressure and malnutrition."

"Malnutrition?" Both Geraldine and Bernice spoke the word at once, equal measures of surprise and disbelief in their voices.

Dana grimaced. "I know. I had the same reaction. The doctor said a lot of older people who live alone suffer from some form of malnutrition. He says they don't want to bother cooking for just one, or they don't feel hungry so they don't eat . . . It makes me feel just awful."

Brian met her eyes again. Across the small distance that separated them, he tried to convey to her the message he knew she needed to hear. This wasn't her fault. Somehow he was sure she felt herself to blame for Ike's health problems.

But before he could say anything to her, someone called her name and she was scurrying across the room to show off one of her designs. Geraldine and Bernice moved after her, eager to see everything in the room.

"Hello, Brian."

Brian turned to find Pualani and Sam Yoshiyama standing beside him.

"That Dana is really something," Sam told Brian, a smile of approval on his face.

Brian, uncertain of what to say to that, remained silent. Pualani gave him a knowing look and began to tell him of the marvelous dress Dana had just delivered.

"I can't wait to wear it to that dinner for the president. The other women are going to be as green as my dress, with envy."

"Dana's very talented," Brian acknowledged.

"Good business sense too," Sam said. He glanced around the store as he sipped from his glass of champagne punch. "This is a very appealing setup. With the restoration work going on, the downtown area is going to be viable again soon. Once word gets around how good she is, people will flock down here. She'll have more business than she and her assistant can handle."

Brian looked around the room again. Sam was right. The soft lighting, the relaxing color of the walls, the casual but attractive furniture—it was all planned to make the women who came in feel comfortable. Then, relaxed, they could choose designs for their wedding gowns and bridesmaids' dresses, or giggle over fabrics for prom gowns.

A new respect for Dana began to grow in Brian. Maybe she had a point when she argued that he looked upon her as a child. He didn't really, of course, but he'd been responsible for Mom and Vovo for so long he felt he had to oversee the affairs of any woman in his life. Mom and Vovo really depended upon him. Dana wouldn't need to.

He was so deep in his thoughts he hardly noticed when Sam and Pualani drifted off to greet someone else.

As the party wound down Brian decided to find Dana and ask her to see him one more time. He had to convince her that he really loved her and that there was hope for their relationship.

He found her smoothing the skirt of a wedding gown she had on display.

"Oh, Brian, you startled me. I was just checking this skirt. For a minute there I thought someone had spilled something on it." She pushed her hair out of her face and straightened up. Her heart was already pounding from the nearness of Brian, but she worked to control it.

"I'd really like to see you, Dana." He ran his fingers through his hair as he watched her brush imaginary lint from the white satin. "We need to talk. Would you come fishing with me on Sunday? I have to work tomorrow."

Dana laughed. The night was going so well. She already had appointments with two prospective brides, and an order for a custom-made muumuu. "I have to work tomorrow too."

Brian smiled down into her eyes. "Of course. How could I forget? You're a businesswoman now." Brian glanced around the large, airy workroom. "Congratulations, Dana. Lokelani's is a great-looking place. You're going to be a big success."

Dana returned the smile. He sure sounded sincere. But she'd been hurt twice already by her feelings for him. Still, she loved to go fishing. It was one of the things they used to do together years ago. And it would be nice to relax after the hectic two weeks she'd just had.

"Thank you, Brian. And yes, I'd like to go fishing on Sunday."

Before anything more could be said, Geraldine and Bernice came over to say good night to Dana and tell Brian they were ready to leave.

Dana turned on the windshield wipers as she drove home Saturday evening. Let it rain now, she thought. The corners of her lips tilted upward as she reviewed the beautiful, sunny day just ending—the first full day of business for Lokelani's.

Engaged women, mothers of brides, and curious browsers had made her first day everything she'd hoped and more. She had another scheduled appointment for a bridal party. With the two from last night that made three! She was so excited she couldn't stop smiling. And the case of gift items was already half depleted. Geraldine and Bernice would be thrilled.

Much as she wanted to go home and mull over her success, Dana knew she'd better stop off at the grocery store and stock up for Ike's return home the next day. The dietitian at the hospital had given her long lists of recommended foods and she wanted to have a wide variety on hand.

The rain had turned into a fitful drizzle by the time Dana pulled into the parking lot at Foodland. The grocery cum drugstore cum dry goods store was fairly busy early on a Saturday evening, forcing Dana to park far from the entrance. As she walked toward the store, she fumbled through her too-full purse looking for the shopping list she knew was in there.

She was almost at the doors when sudden shouts erupted, distracting her from her search for the list and bringing her full attention to the store entrance. People, both customers and employees, were literally running from the large double doors, pouring out into the parking lot and stopping in little groups around her, exchanging frantic stories. Dana joined the nearest group to listen in. Perhaps the store was on fire.

What she heard was jumbled and contradictory. Several people had seen a strange-looking man weaving through the store aisles. A middle-aged woman was shaking her head as she described the "hippie" that she just knew was going to be trouble.

Dana scanned the now sizable group of people standing outside the store. There must be someone here she knew who could tell her what was happening.

Finally she saw her neighbor's daughter, and she pushed her way over to her side.

"Connie, what's going on?"

"Dana." The young woman in the blue apron with the supermarket's logo on it turned and gave her a fierce hug. "Oh, I'm so sorry."

Dana returned the hug but couldn't understand what Connie could be so sorry about. Ike had been back for a week. Surely she wasn't just now offering sympathy for his disappearance?

As she pulled back from the embrace, Dana

noticed the tears dampening the other woman's eyes. "Oh, Connie. What is it?"

"There's some weird guy in there, over at the pharmacy. He grabbed a little kid and was waving a gun around."

She pulled Dana back into a fierce hug that once again set her wondering. But Connie's next words brought understanding.

"Brian is in there with him, Dana. He was just going in when this all started, and he's still in there."

Dana thought certainly her heart had stopped beating. Something was going on in the store—a robbery or something involving a man everyone agreed looked very strange. A man with a gun. And Brian was in there with him.

A truth she'd been reluctant to face hit her with hurricane force. She loved Brian. The thought of him in there facing unknown dangers was so painful . . . It was like losing Ike all over again.

She apparently turned white enough to frighten her friend. Connie took her arm and led her over to the cement curb where she urged her to sit and lower her head between her knees.

"It's okay," she told her, over and over again. "He's a cop, he'll know what to do. He'll be okay."

Dana swallowed. Reassuring Connie that she was all right, she pushed herself up, managing to stand on shaky knees. Two police cars and a fire engine entered the parking lot, one rapidly following the other. As she and Connie held on to each other while watching the activity around the store, she clung to the hope that Connie was right. Brian would know what to do. Brian would be okay.

Inside the building, Brian remained calm.

He'd had a hectic day at work. Four teenagers—three boys and one girl—had been arrested late last night. They felt sure the four teens were the gang responsible for the robberies in the subdivisions off Komohana. They had to get search warrants for each of the kids' homes, then sort through all the stuff they'd found, matching items to things missing from the various houses that had been robbed.

All he'd wanted to do this evening was go home and relax. Maybe watch an old movie on television.

But Vovo had called just before he left the station, asking him to stop at Foodland to pick up her "pressure pills."

He'd headed straight for the pharmacy section of the store, anxious to get the pills and go on home. But he was still short of the pharmacy when he noticed a long-haired man, probably in his early twenties and wearing only a pair of worn and dirty jeans, weaving back and forth through the store's aisles. His eyes were wide and unfocused, making Brian wonder if he was high on drugs. He'd moved forward to intercept him when the younger man started to run, grabbed hold of a nearby toddler, and dashed behind the counter of the pharmacy.

Brian stood now with the nearly hysterical mother of the small child who was wiggling and screaming in the stranger's hold. The young man faced the white-haired pharmacist, reaching into the pocket of his jeans for a small gun. With a shaky hand, he trained it on the pharmacist. Brian couldn't hear him over the child's wails but he was sure he'd demanded drugs.

The startled pharmacist, an elderly man Brian had known for years and who was just months away from retirement, looked ready to pass out. The mother of the little boy now screaming in the arms of the would-be thief started screaming herself.

In seconds, the whole store was in chaos. Taking control of the situation, Brian managed to send some of the store customers out, directing them to tell anyone else they encountered on their way outside to leave also.

The child's mother he kept beside him. He

tried to soothe her but she was rapidly becoming hysterical. So he took her shoulders in his hands and gave her a sharp shake.

"You have to stay calm, for the sake of your son."

He watched with relief as the woman swallowed, then nodded. She reached into a large handbag for a wad of tissues which she used to mop her face. Then she drew in a large hiccuping breath as her eyes pleaded with Brian.

"Okay. That's better." He tried to smile his reassurance. "Let me talk to him. Maybe I can get him to release the baby."

She squeezed his arm in silent gratitude as she looked between him and her child.

Brian covered her hand with his. "You stay here. I'll see what I can do."

Brian moved closer to the counter, keeping his hands out where the robber could see them. The perpetrator was staring frantically around the store. Brian could make out screams and shouts from the store customers and employees, but he didn't think the other man could hear anything over the child's screams. Maybe it was the motion of the people leaving the building that had attracted his attention.

Brian was up to the counter now, directly opposite the man holding the screaming child. He raised his voice to be sure the other man would be able to hear him.

"Why don't you let me have the child?" Even at the increased volume level he managed to keep his voice calm. And he remained standing, unmoving, his hands resting on the countertop. If this man was on a bad drug trip it would not be a good idea to make sudden moves. His finger was on the trigger of the small gun and his hand didn't look any too steady.

"Give him to his mother. Then he'll stop crying."

Something about the calm voice apparently got through. The perpetrator looked over at the woman still clutching her handful of tissues and motioned with his head for her to come closer.

"Come around here and take him," he shouted. "He's making me deaf."

Brian remained where he was, trying to keep the stranger's attention focused on himself. The woman had taken her son and backed off, getting as far as she could from her son's attacker. The child was still sobbing, but at least the screaming had stopped.

"Let them go," Brian repeated. "The old man too." He nodded toward Mr. Akana, the pharmacist. "I'll stay with you, be your hostage."

The perpetrator shook his head, making his

long hair fly. He blinked once, then looked between Brian and Mr. Akana. "You're trying to confuse me. Just let me think."

Brian kept his head facing forward, his eyes locked on the perpetrator. But he'd moved one hand below the counter and was gesturing to the young mother, indicating she should head for the nearby aisle and get out of sight. She seemed to understand what he was trying to convey. Slowly she rocked her son against her chest, crooning softly to him, all the while inching backward.

The perpetrator was still staring at the pharmacist. Thinking was hard work for him in his present state.

"I want amphetamines and barbiturates. I need him to get them."

"He's an old man. He looks a little green. He might be having a heart attack. You wouldn't want him to die on you." Brian tried to catch the eye of Mr. Akana, wondering if he realized what he was hinting at.

Right on cue, Mr. Akana pressed his hand to his chest and took a shallow breath that rattled in his throat.

Brian decided to press while he could. He could no longer see the mother and child in his peripheral vision, and he hoped they were finally out of sight between the tall shelves of products.

"Let me go back there with you. Mr. Akana can tell me where the stuff you want is located. I can get it for you."

Brian hoped the thief wasn't sufficiently alert to realize that Mr. Akana could just tell him where to go to help himself.

The thief looked from one to the other once more, then jerked his head violently, first toward Brian, then away. "Okay. Come on back here."

He gestured with the gun, causing Brian to hold his breath as the unsteady hand thrust forward.

"You." He motioned toward Mr. Akana. "Tell him where it is." He twisted his head back and forth again, trying to keep both men in his vision. "Be quick about it."

Then the strange young man looked about, rotating his whole body this time, turning on the balls of his bare feet as he tried to look over the tops of the shelves. His voice rose to a shrill whine.

"Where is she? What happened to the kid?"

Outside the store the police were conferring with the store managers. Officers disappeared inside and didn't return. Dana and Connie stayed together—having a friend nearby helped ease the anxiety.

Suddenly a young woman holding a crying child came dashing through the open doors. She looked ready to collapse as the police met her there and ushered her over to a paramedic unit.

Murmurs traveled quickly through the crowd.

"That's the child," Connie told Dana. "The one that weirdo grabbed before he pulled the gun."

Dana sucked in her breath.

Brian had done it. She knew he had. He'd talked the man out of using the child as a hostage. She was proud of him.

But did that mean he himself was in greater danger?

She loved Brian. She could admit it now; she just hoped it wasn't too late for them. She'd spent these past weeks denying her love because of fear, she now realized. She was afraid to trust someone so much—to give someone else so much control over her life.

It was time to admit to herself that she was in love with Brian. Probably always had been. They complemented each other and belonged together. There would be some mistakes. She grimaced as she thought of his attempt to put

Ike in a home. But she realized now that it was well-meant. He was trying to take care of them both in a manner he thought best.

Dana smiled. She'd just have to educate him in certain areas.

She was feeling better when she heard it.

Everyone else heard it too. The crowd became eerily quiet. Police rushed into the building.

It sounded like firecrackers exploding. And it came from inside the store.

Chapter Ten

The gunman swung around wildly when he realized he'd lost his best hostages. His flying hand tightened on the trigger, sending two shots into the ceiling.

Brian saw his chance. He bolted over the counter, landing on his feet behind the perp. One arm went around the man's bare torso, and he stretched his other arm out, trying to grasp the hand that held the gun. Unable to reach the thrashing arm, he forced their bodies into a turn, trying to keep the gun away from the cringing figure of Mr. Akana.

Brian had him now and knew he could hold him until help arrived. He could already see officers rushing forward from two different directions.

But the perpetrator became even more frantic when he realized he'd been caught; he squeezed the trigger again and again as he flailed. Four more shots rang out, flying into the pharmacy shelves, knocking plastic bottles into the wall and onto the floor, before the other officers were able to reach Brian and help bring the man under control. Thankfully, no one was hurt by the wild shots.

As Brian moved toward Mr. Akana to see if the old man was all right, he looked down the long aisle that led to the store entrance. A crowd of people stood out there, behind a temporary barricade. And right there in front, he saw a petite woman, in a bright pink muumuu, with short curling dark hair.

He stopped. Dana was out there, had apparently been out there for some time. Had she been in the store when the guy entered? Did she know he was inside?

Dana saw Brian at the same moment he saw her. Across the long length of the store aisle, their eyes locked for the merest moment and something electric traveled between them. Dana's heart lurched in her chest. She needed a deep breath, but she managed to smile. It was all right. Brian was okay.

* * *

It was some time before Brian could leave the store to look for Dana. It was probably only fifteen or twenty minutes in actual time, but to Brian it felt like hours. He'd gotten just that brief glimpse of Dana, yet he knew something important had happened in that visual exchange.

Finally, he was able to walk out of the store.

And there she was, standing at the front of the crowd, waiting for him. He stopped a few feet away and held out his arms.

He wasn't disappointed. Dana flew into them, throwing her arms around his neck and burying her face in his shoulder.

The crowd, which had grown since Dana first arrived, applauded. There were good-natured hoots and yells of encouragement.

Brian and Dana didn't hear a thing. Their eyes, their ears, all of their senses, were aware only of that one other person.

"Oh, Brian. Thank heavens you're all right."

Brian held her for a long moment before releasing her enough to look into her eyes. "I love you, Dana."

"I love you too." Dana looked into Brian's eyes and her voice softened. "And I'm so proud of you."

Brian gathered her close and lowered his lips to hers. The crowd cheered.

Dana felt warmed and protected in Brian's strong arms. His kiss created a flutter in her belly that was both comforting and frustrating at the same time. But the terrible knot of fear was gone.

Brian drew Dana closer, relishing the feel of her softness against him. For a brief instant earlier that evening, he had wondered if he'd ever see her again. His lips left hers and he brought his hand up to brush away the wisps of hair feathering across her cheeks.

"I was afraid I might die without ever having the chance to tell you how much I love you."

Dana melted against him. "Oh, Brian. I love you so much. I was so worried."

Late that night, driving home, the groceries finally chosen and stored in the car, Dana reflected on her cherished independence. Here she was, ready to marry Brian and spend the rest of her life with him. Which meant herself and Brian, Ike, Geraldine, and Bernice. A houseful! And she didn't even care.

In fact, she was already looking at the good side. She wouldn't have to do much cooking or cleaning—between the three older people all the small everyday stuff would be taken care of. She could even think about having children, with so many willing baby-sitters available if she wanted to continue working.

Dana smiled to herself as she pulled the car into the carport. Apparently she'd done some growing up in these last few weeks. As she entered the house with the last of the groceries and locked the door behind her, she felt the loneliness of the empty house for the first time. Ike was coming home tomorrow. She couldn't wait to share her news.

"What do you mean you won't live with us?" Dana had driven Ike home and helped him get comfortable on the living room couch. Now she stood beside him, clearly upset by his earlier statement.

"Brian already has a houseful. I'll be fine right here. And I'm very happy for you."

Dana clenched her teeth as she stared at her dad. He'd always been stubborn. She knew he would get upset if she told him he couldn't manage on his own. And after all they'd just been through, she couldn't bear to upset him. So she remained silent.

The smell of fresh coffee tickled Dana awake. She blinked against the early morning brightness and sniffed again. What . . . ?

She found Ike in the kitchen already dressed

and pouring himself a cup of coffee. Half a papaya and two slices of whole-wheat toast awaited him at his place on the table.

"Dad, what are you doing?" Dana pulled out a chair and sat at the table, propping her elbows up in front of her and resting her head on both her hands. "I was going to get your breakfast."

Ike returned the pot to the stove and sat down. "I'm having my breakfast," he replied to her earlier question. He took a sip of his coffee and gave her a smile of pure contentment. "Mmm, that's good. But don't worry. It's decaf. But it sure is nice to do for myself again."

He buttered a slice of toast. "See this? Whole-wheat bread and low-fat margarine." He took a bite. "Not too bad, either. Especially since I was able to fix it myself." He replaced the piece of toast on his plate and put his hand on Dana's shoulder. "Don't worry, honey. I've learned my lesson. I know now that I have to pay attention to meals if I want to stay healthy. I'll be real careful."

Dana stared at him, wondering if she was still asleep and dreaming all this. All these years she'd been so concerned about her own independence. And it appeared Ike felt the same way about his own. He may have wanted her to live in her old home, but he wasn't anxious to have someone else do everything for him. He wanted to do for himself everything that he was capable of.

And she had no doubt he was capable of a lot. Right now he was reaping such enjoyment from the simple act of preparing his own breakfast. A smile suffused her own face as she watched him. It was going to be all right after all. Until she and Brian came to a decision about marrying, she and Ike would share the house, but live their own lives.

When she tuned back in to the conversation, Ike was asking if she'd be home for dinner.

"I'm making chicken. They gave me some menus and recipes at the hospital. Sound pretty good too."

"That sounds great, Dad. Can you make enough for three?" A smile tipped her lips as she remembered the fishing date she had with Brian that afternoon. She'd bring him back for dinner.

She left Ike busily checking his recipes while she went back to her room to change. When she returned to the kitchen, it was empty. Ike had said something about a walk. She hoped he wouldn't overdo it.

She was finishing her orange juice and laughing over the comics from the Sunday *Advertiser* when she heard the front door open.

"Dana." Ike's voice carried clearly through the house.

Leaving the newspaper on the table, she hurried into the living room to see what her dad might want. Maybe the walk was too much for him after all, and he needed her help. Her step quickened.

"Brian!"

"Surprised you, didn't I?" Ike stood beside Brian, grinning like a small child. "Met him in the driveway, just as I was getting back."

Dana smiled shyly at Brian. He held a long white florist's box in his hands, and she found herself momentarily tongue-tied.

Ike, still with a silly grin on his face, excused himself and disappeared into his bedroom. "Have to get my rest, you know," he said as he shut the door noisily behind him. Within a minute the sweet strains of slack-key guitar music could be heard behind the door.

Brian and Dana grinned at one another. "It seems to be our destiny to be thrown together by older relatives," Brian remarked. He drew Dana over to the sofa and sat down beside her. He put the florist's box down on his other side while he greeted Dana properly with a lingering kiss. Then he opened the box, parted the tissue, and removed a fragrant white floral lei.

"Two years ago, Dana, I offered you my love

and a pikake lei. I was going to ask you to marry me." Brian's eyes searched Dana's face before he continued. "I can't promise you a smooth and carefree life, Dana. I know that now. But I will try to make you happy. And I can promise you all my love. Forever."

Tears dampened Dana's eyes, making them bright as she smiled at Brian. He lifted the lei in his hands and placed it around her neck. Then he kissed her gently on her lips.

"Dana, I'm going to try again. Will you marry me?"

Dana smiled, a bright happy smile. She threw her arms around Brian and hugged him, heedless of the fragile blossoms that crushed between them, shedding their delicate perfume.

"Yes. Definitely yes." She backed away so she could look up at him. Her voice was soft. "Thank you."

Brian looked puzzled.

Dana smiled. "For giving me another chance."

The guitar music grew louder. Ike's head peeked out around the edge of his bedroom door. "Did you say yes?"

Dana had to laugh. "Yes, Dad. I did."

"Good. Always knew you were a smart girl." Then he turned around, reentered the bedroom, and closed the door. Within seconds, the door reopened. "What are you waiting for? Give each other a kiss."

Brian and Dana laughed, but went into each other's arms, happy to comply. They didn't hear Ike's chuckle, or the noisy click as the door closed once more.

Behind the bedroom door, the music stopped in mid-note. When it started up again the new tune was the "Hawaiian Wedding Song."